JACOB A. SANSOUCIE

Moonshine & Blood

To my wonderful mother. With Love.

Contents

Acknowledgments

Though I am a die-hard fantasy nerd at heart, my love for history has always been just as strong. Writing *Moonshine & Blood* has been a passion project—one that allowed me to blend storytelling with the rich and rugged past of the Ozarks. While this is a work of fiction, I aimed to stay as historically authentic as possible, with a few creative liberties taken for the sake of narrative flow.

I owe a tremendous debt of gratitude to those who lent their expertise in ensuring the historical elements of this book remained accurate and immersive:

- **Tom Koob**, author of several books on Ozarks history, whose insights helped refine and authenticate the historical details.
- **Susan Croce Kelly** (*www.susancrocekelly.com*), whose expertise and guidance were invaluable in shaping the historical accuracy of this story.

A heartfelt thank you to my incredible **Beta Readers**, whose thoughtful feedback and keen observations helped shape this novel into what it is today:

- **Sherry Bass**
- **Jennifer Luko**
- **Connie Timpson**
- **Taylor Coleman**

- **Casey Rene Slovensky**

And to those who contributed their time and insight but preferred to remain anonymous, I deeply appreciate your help as well.

To everyone who supported this journey, whether through encouragement, critique, or simply a shared love of storytelling—thank you.

It is with great pleasure that I present *Moonshine & Blood*, and I hope you enjoy the ride.

— Jacob SanSoucie

1

The Iron Horse Home

The morning sun painted long shadows through the Ozark valleys as the Frisco cut its iron path through the highlands, steam and coal smoke trailing behind like the train's own private cloud. The July heat pressed heavy in the passenger car, despite the open windows that let in whatever breeze the train's movement could catch. Ladies fanned themselves with folded newspapers, and men's collar points had long since wilted in the humidity.

Jesse Walker sat in the worn leather seat, his shirt already damp between his shoulder blades. He'd propped his weathered boots on his canvas rucksack, losing himself in Thoreau's words about a man's duty to his conscience. The book's spine was cracked from repeated readings, its pages dog-eared from years of contemplation. Every few minutes, he'd shift position, unsticking himself from the leather seat.

The first whiff of trouble came with the reek of cheap whiskey and cheaper cologne, made worse by the summer heat. Two seats ahead, a red-faced man in an ill-fitting suit swayed into the aisle, his face shining with sweat, fixing bleary eyes on a young mother trying to quiet her frightened child.

"Ain't you just the prettiest thing…" The drunk slurred, dropping heavy hands onto their seat back.

Jesse marked his page with a deliberate motion, rising slowly from his seat. "Might want to find yourself a seat, friend. Mornin's an ill-suited time for such foolishness."

The drunk spun, nearly losing his balance. "Mind your own… business, boy."

"That's precisely what I'm tryin' to do," Jesse replied, holding up his book. "But you're makin' it mighty difficult for folks to tend to theirs."

The man lunged with a haymaker that would have been telegraphed in the previous century. Jesse sidestepped, letting momentum carry his opponent past. A quick strike to the man's midsection doubled him over, and as he stumbled forward, Jesse's follow-up blow to the back of his leg sent him sprawling. Jesse caught him before he hit the floor, easing him into an empty seat with the practiced efficiency of someone who'd done this dance before.

The commotion had drawn the conductor, who'd witnessed the latter half of the confrontation from the adjacent car. After the drunk had been safely restrained and deposited in one of the rear cars, the conductor approached Jesse with an appraising look. "Mind following me for a moment, son?"

Jesse gathered his belongings and followed the railman through the swaying passenger cars, his actions drawing respectful nods from other travelers.

The caboose was a study in the efficient use of space. Polished brass hardware gleamed against dark wood panels, and the morning light streamed through the cupola windows above. The conductor's desk, a masterpiece of railway engineering, folded down from the wall on brass hinges, its surface covered in dispatch orders and train schedules.

"Make yourself comfortable," the conductor said, gesturing to a well-worn leather chair. His eyes flickered to Jesse's military pack as he set it down. He retrieved a pair of cigars from an ornate humidor, extending one toward Jesse. "Figured you might appreciate something better than that army-issued tobacky."

Jesse accepted with a grateful nod, savoring the rich tobacco as the conductor poured two cups of coffee from a battered pot that lived atop the small pot-bellied stove.

"Noticed you reading when all that started," the conductor said, settling into his chair. "Don't see many folks out here with their nose in books. Most just stare out windows." He paused, taking a sip of coffee. "You serve in the Great War?"

"Yes sir. 35th Infantry Division," Jesse replied quietly, watching the smoke curl toward the ceiling. "Missouri National Guard."

"Saint-Mihiel? Meuse-Argonne?"

Jesse nodded, his eyes distant. "Both. Stayed on after the surrender, servin' as a clerk for Third Army during the armistice."

"Where you headed now?" the conductor asked, settling deeper into his chair.

"Back home," Jesse said. "Family farm outside Ozark."

"Ozark?" The conductor tamped his cigar on a brass ashtray. "That's a long time to be away from home after the war."

"Didn't feel right comin' straight home, I needed to sort things out," Jesse said, his eyes distant. "Spent some time travelin' through France and Belgium after my clerk duties. Figured I ought to see those places when they weren't on fire." He paused, turning the cigar in his fingers. "Walked the streets of Paris, saw the rebuilding in Verdun. Just wanted to see what France looked like without the gunfire and artillery."

The conductor nodded knowingly. "Well, the Ozarks have sorted themselves out too, though not all for the better. Prohibition's hit the farmers hard - they haven't been able to sell their corn to the whiskey makers for a few years now. Some are turning to other means, if you take my meaning." He paused, checking his pocket watch. "We'll be pulling into Frisco Station in Springfield in about two hours. Lot's changed since you left, son, but those hills still stand just like they always have."

Jesse gazed out the window at the passing landscape, the familiar hills rising through the morning mist. "Some things don't change," he agreed softly. He paused, watching the hills, then added quietly, "But some things change a man forever."

The conductor studied him for a moment, then busied himself with his paperwork, leaving Jesse to his thoughts and the comfort of good tobacco as the train wound its way home.

* * *

The train's brakes squealed as it eased into Frisco Station, the red brick building with its fresh green awnings coming into view. Jesse watched passengers surge forward and back on the platform like waves against a shore, their voices mixing with the hiss of steam and clatter of luggage carts. Slinging his canvas military bag over his shoulder, he made his way through the station, noting how the old oil lanterns had given way to electric bulbs that cast a harsh, steady light across the polished floors.

Main Street stopped him in his tracks. Automobiles puttered between horse-drawn wagons, their horns mixing with the clip-clop of hooves. Prohibition flyers adorned every lamppost, their stern warnings impossible to miss. Jesse pulled out his father's pocket watch, the silver case worn smooth from three generations of hands. Despite its age, it still kept accurate time, which served him well in the trenches of France.

A newsboy on the corner caught his eye. "Any good news worth tellin' these days?" Jesse asked.

"Mister, good news costs two pennies!" The boy shot back, quick as a whip.

Jesse laughed, fishing the coins from his pocket. "Mark Twain once said newspapers are for people who can't think for themselves…though I suspect he'd have bought one anyway." Taking his paper, he settled onto a bench in front of the station, his eyes drawn to the Richmond Bank and Trust. The old Springfield Mercantile Bank's familiar facade had been transformed by recent renovations, its limestone gleaming in the morning sun.

The headlines in the Springfield Leader jumped out at him: federal threats about prohibition enforcement, the prolonged strike of the Missouri and North Arkansas Railroad, and M.E. Gillioz's ambitious plans for a theater. Before he could read further, a car's distinctive put-put drew near.

"Cousin Jesse! What a pleasure to see you back home!"

Jesse looked up to see Luke, transformed from the reserved boy he remembered into a well-dressed lawyer. His cousin's suit probably cost more than most folks made in a month, and the Model T shined like it had just rolled off Ford's assembly line.

"Luke Walker," Jesse stood, embracing his cousin. "Well now, ain't you grown into quite the prosperous gentleman."

"We've all progressed," Luke said smoothly, taking Jesse's duffle with manicured hands. "Even our beloved Ozarks are finally embracing modernity." He placed the bag carefully in the motorcar. "Shall we depart?"

* * *

They drove south down Campbell Street, the Model T's engine chugging steadily. A Ford TT bus pulled out from the Bus Barn, its larger frame dwarfing their automobile. A cable car clanged past, its bell echoing off the buildings.

"That's the newly constructed Ullman Hotel," Luke gestured toward an impressive structure, his voice carrying that carefully cultivated tone he'd developed since law school. "They're saying it shall transform our region into a genuine tourist destination. The Ozarks are finally receiving their due recognition."

Jesse nodded, studying his cousin's manicured hands on the steering wheel - so different from the boy who'd once helped him mend fences on the farm. Back then, Luke had thrown himself into every chore, as if trying to earn his place at the Walker table.

His attention caught on the shuttered storefronts, their windows plastered with foreclosure notices. "Mason's Hardware... Old man Mason fixed my first bicycle when I was just a boy. Thompson's Grocery too."

"Progress is inevitable, dear cousin." Luke's said. "Some individuals simply cannot adapt to modern times."

"Progress shouldn't mean destroyin' good folks' livelihoods," Jesse said quietly.

The city gave way to farmland, rows of wheat and corn swaying in the summer breeze. The familiar scent of fresh-cut hay and wild honeysuckle brought back memories of running through these same fields as a boy.

"Jesse," Luke's voice grew serious. "I must express my deepest condolences regarding Uncle James."

Jesse turned sharply. "What about Father?"

Luke's fingers tightened on the steering wheel. "The letters... did you receive them?"

"What letters?"

"I'm sorry to inform you, cousin. Your father passed away four months ago. They discovered him near Finley Cave. Appears he fell, broke his neck."

Jesse stared out at the passing wheat fields, his throat tight. His hand went to the pocket watch, feeling its familiar weight. The last time he'd seen his father, they'd fought about his enlistment. James Walker had called him a fool for running off to fight someone else's war.

"I apologize," Luke said, something of the old boy showing through his polished exterior. "I didn't intend to deliver such news so abruptly."

"You couldn't have known I didn't know." Jesse's voice was steady, but his knuckles were white around the watch.

"Have you eaten today? We could stop at the diner in Ozark before heading to the farm. There are some matters we should discuss before you return home."

"No, I haven't eaten." Jesse kept his eyes on the fields, watching them roll past like the French countryside. "A meal would be fine enough, but if it comes with more ill tidings, I'd sooner go hungry."

"In my experience," said Luke, adjusting his cuffs, "bad news is easier to digest over a good meal."

* * *

Luke turned onto a gravel drive alongside the Finley River, kicking up dust as it approached the Riverside Inn. The newly constructed lodge stood proud against the backdrop of oak trees, its fresh-cut timber walls still holding that clean pine scent. Green canvas canopies fluttered over each window and the main entrance, providing shade from the Missouri summer sun.

Jesse noticed several automobiles and a couple of wagons parked out front, a testament to the establishment's growing popularity. A cool breeze from the Finley River cut through the summer heat, carrying with it the sweet scent of water and river-worn sycamores. The sound of running water mixed with laughter and conversation drifting from the open windows.

"*Chicken Dinners Served Daily,*" Jesse read the hand-painted sign out front. "Haven't had proper chicken since before France," Jesse mused.

"Army cuisine could make a buzzard reconsider its career choices."

"Well cousin, you're in for quite the experience," Luke said as he parked the motorcar. "Mrs. Garrison raises her own chickens, and her cornbread could make a grown man cry."

The scent of fried chicken and fresh-baked bread wafted out as they approached the entrance. Through the windows, Jesse could see tables filled with locals – farmers taking a break from their fields, businessmen from town, and families gathering for a late lunch. The dining room's polished wood floors glistened in the afternoon light streaming through the windows.

A young waitress with auburn hair tied back in a blue ribbon led them to a corner table near the window. Something about her smile tugged at Jesse's memory.

"Jesse Walker?" Her eyes lit up. "You probably don't remember me - Jenny Winters? I used to help your sister Mary with the chickens sometimes. My daddy had the farm next to Peterson's orchard?"

Recognition dawned. "Jenny? Lord, you were just a little thing when I left." Jesse smiled warmly. "How's your folks?"

"Moved to Springfield couple years back. I'm stayin' with my aunt, workin' here while I save up some money." She touched the blue ribbon in her hair. "My mama made this outta one of her old dresses before they left."

"It's lovely," Jesse said softly. "Put me in mind of those wild cornflowers near our camp in France."

Jenny's smile brightened at that. "Thank ya kindly. Now, what can I get for you both?"

Luke smoothed his tie and picked up the menu written in chalk on a small blackboard. "I'll have the chicken dinner, extra cornbread if you please, green beans on the side, and some sweet iced tea."

Jesse studied the offerings, inhaling the aroma of pepper and sage drifting from the kitchen. "Same for me, ma'am, though I'd be obliged if you'd add some of those fine-smellin' mashed potatoes. And coffee, if you please - black as midnight."

Jenny nodded and hurried toward the kitchen, her ribbon trailing behind her.

Jesse took a sip of water, his jaw tightening like a rifle bolt. "Well then, might as well face this head-on. What else you got weighin' on your mind?"

Luke's fingers drummed against the white tablecloth. He straightened his tie, avoiding Jesse's gaze. "Jesse, there's a delicate situation regarding the farm. Since your father's passing, Aunt Sarah hasn't been able to maintain the loan payments. I've offered my assistance, but she's declined. The bank…" he paused, choosing his words carefully, "is running out of patience."

Jesse's hand froze halfway to his water glass. "Hold on now - since when was there a loan? My grandfather cleared that debt before he passed. That land's been Walker ground for four generations."

"Well, shortly after you went to war, The Ozarks experienced a terrible drought. Uncle James had to secure a loan from the bank to preserve the farm. Since his passing, the payments have fallen behind."

Jesse leaned back in his chair, the wood creaking beneath him. His fingers traced the edge of his father's pocket watch as his mind raced through the implications. The farm was supposed to be their anchor, their bedrock – and now he discovered it's been mortgaged without a word to him. His family had faced this crisis alone while he was overseas, and they never mentioned a word to him.

The front door's bell chimed and Sheriff Marcus Hayes walked in, his weathered face breaking into smiles as he greeted the lunch crowd. His badge caught the sunlight as he moved, the silver star worn smooth from years of service. The gun belt rode low on his hip, leather cracked but well-maintained like everything else about him.

Luke's earlier confidence crumbled at the sight of Hayes, and Jesse remembered that rainy morning all those years ago - Hayes standing in their farmhouse kitchen, hat in hand, telling thirteen-year-old Luke about finding his mother dead in a boarding house in Springfield. Sarah had held Luke for hours that day while he didn't shed a single tear, he just stared out the window at the rain.

Hayes stopped mid-stride when he spotted Jesse. "Well good Lord almighty, if it ain't Jesse Walker! Finally made your way back home to us, have ya?"

Jesse stood as Hayes approached their table, accepting the older man's bearlike embrace. The familiar scent of leather and pipe tobacco brought back memories of summer evenings on the porch, Hayes and his father sharing stories while Jesse sat at their feet.

"Just look at you now," Hayes stepped back, keeping his hands on Jesse's shoulders like a proud uncle might. "Grown into a fine man. Your daddy woulda burst his buttons with pride seein' you now. Lord knows he did anyway, every time I'd bring him them newspaper articles 'bout your unit."

Jesse remembered the sheriff bringing by newspapers and letters during his childhood, staying for supper more often than not. Hayes had been there for every important moment - teaching Jesse to shoot, helping patch the barn roof, even bailing him out that time he and Mary got caught stealing apples from old man Peterson's orchard.

Luke shifted in his chair, his fingers tapping an anxious rhythm against his water glass.

"My contract with Uncle Sam ran its course a couple years ago," Jesse said simply. "After that, I needed to see those French cities when they weren't on fire, walk their streets in peace. But eventually, a man's got to come back to his own soil."

"You done us proud over there, son. Kept track of every word written about your outfit." Hayes's expression softened. "And Jesse... about your daddy. That loss... well, it shook this whole community somethin' fierce. James and me, we was like brothers since we was boys - ain't been the same 'round here without him."

"Thank you, sir." Jesse's throat tightened as Hayes gave his shoulder a final pat.

The sheriff tipped his hat. "Luke," he said coolly, before heading toward his usual table by the kitchen.

Jesse settled back into his chair, studying Luke's face. His cousin's earlier confidence had evaporated the moment Hayes walked in, replaced by a nervous energy that set Jesse's combat-honed instincts on edge.

"What's troublin' you, Luke?" Jesse asked. "You've had the look of a man standin' on quicksand since Hayes walked in."

Luke smoothed his tie with practiced precision, a gesture Jesse remembered from their childhood whenever Luke felt cornered. "The sheriff and I have had some... professional disagreements lately. Legal matters." His voice carried that careful tone he'd cultivated in law school. "Small towns have long memories, cousin." There was something in his tone that reminded Jesse of those nights he'd found Luke in the barn, poring over his mother's old letters by lamplight.

The floorboards creaked behind them as their waitress approached, bearing two steaming plates. The aroma of perfectly fried chicken and fresh herbs filled the air.

"But that's hardly proper lunch conversation," Luke said, his eyes flickering toward Hayes's table before returning to methodically arrange his silverware, each piece aligned just so.

* * *

The drive to the Walker Farm stretched in silence, broken only by the Model T's puttering engine and the crunch of gravel and dirt under its wheels. Jesse watched the passing landscape, his father's pocket watch heavy in his palm. Luke's earlier unease around Sheriff Hayes nagged at him, but Jesse pushed the thought aside. His time in the trenches had taught him the value of patience – some secrets revealed themselves only when ready.

The sweet, earthy scent of ripening corn drifted through the open window as Luke steered the car off the main road. They passed under the weather-worn wooden sign that had welcomed Jesse home countless times before: "Walker Farms," its letters faded but still proud against the weathered wood.

Tall corn stalks lined both sides of the dirt drive, their green leaves swaying in the afternoon breeze. The familiar sight brought a tightness to Jesse's chest – how many times had he walked these rows with his father, learning the secrets of the soil?

As they rounded the final bend, Jesse spotted a figure in the field. Mary, his kid sister - barely twenty-four now - stood knee-deep in the irrigation ditch, her hat tilted against the sun as she worked to clear debris from the channel. She'd traded her old dress for modified men's work clothes, practical for the heavy farm work she'd taken on. She paused, leaning on her rake, as the Model T's engine announced their approach.

The old farmhouse stood proud despite its weathered appearance. White paint peeled from the clapboard siding like old scars, and the wraparound porch sagged slightly at the corners. Yet the bones were strong – built by Jesse's great-grandfather with oak cut from their own land. Morning glories still climbed the porch columns, just as they had when Jesse was a boy.

Sarah Walker stood in the doorway, one hand pressed against the frame. Her work-worn fingers trembled as she spotted Jesse, and the lines around her eyes deepened with emotion. The gray in her hair had spread since he'd left, streaking through what was once rich chestnut brown, now pulled back in a practical bun at her nape. Her dress, a faded blue cotton that had seen better days, hung loose on her frame, but her dark brown eyes held the same fierce love they always had. Though barely in her fifties, the past few years had aged her beyond her years.

"Jesse? My boy, is that you?" The screen door banged shut behind her as she hurried down the steps, her sensible shoes clattering against the wood. She threw her arms around him, her tears dampening his shirt collar. "My boy is home, my sweet baby is home."

"It's alright, Mama, I'm home now, everything will be fine." Jesse stroked her hair, breathing in the familiar scent of lye soap and fresh bread that always clung to her.

The crunch of boots on gravel announced Mary's approach from the fields. She'd grown into a woman during his absence, though her features still held echoes of the teenage sister he'd left behind. Her blonde hair escaping from its tight braid, caught the sunlight like wheat ready for harvest. Dust and sweat streaked her tanned face, and her man's work shirt was rolled up at the sleeves, revealing strong forearms carned from years of taking on their father's duties. Their father's eyes stared out from her face - that same storm-cloud gray - but now they fixed on Jesse with an unreadable expression.

Without a word, she crossed her arms and stalked into the house, letting the screen door slam behind her. The sound cut through the afternoon quiet like a gunshot. Jesse held his mother tighter, feeling the sharp edges of her shoulder blades through her dress.

* * *

Jesse opened the old door to his childhood bedroom. His mother had preserved it like a museum piece – the same faded quilt on the narrow bed, his dog-eared books still lined up on the shelf, and even his old hunting rifle mounted above the dresser. The room smelled of cedar and memories.

He caught his reflection in the old mirror above the washbasin – same dark hair and brown eyes as his mother, though the war had left its mark. At twenty-seven, his lean face carried more years than it should, and his tall frame held the rigid bearing of a soldier that civilian life hadn't quite softened. The evening sun through the window caught the small scar above his left eye, a souvenir from the Argonne that hadn't been there when he'd last stood in this room.

After washing up and changing into fresh clothes, Jesse tucked away his belongings into his footlocker. In his hand, he held a small leather bag as he made his way down to the sitting room.

Mary sat by the open window, still in her dirt-streaked work clothes. The newspaper Jesse had bought earlier rustled in her grip as she pretended to read, though her eyes weren't moving across the page. The lantern beside her cast dancing shadows across her face, highlighting the stubborn set of her jaw – so much like their father's.

Through the kitchen doorway, Jesse could hear his mother moving about, the familiar rhythm of her footsteps mixing with the clink of dishes. The house felt smaller than he remembered, or maybe he'd just grown bigger.

Jesse settled into the chair opposite Mary, feeling the warm summer breeze drift through the open windows. The curtains swayed gently, carrying the night sounds of crickets and distant whip-poor-wills. The air moved through the house like a living thing, stirring papers and cooling the rooms still holding the day's heat.

Mary turned another page with more force than necessary, her silence a wall between them as solid as any trench barrier Jesse had encountered in France.

Jesse reached into his leather bag and pulled out an ornate smoking pipe, a treasure he'd found in a small shop in Paris. The worn brass fittings caught the lantern light as he retrieved his tin of Bull Durham, the familiar tobacco that had kept many soldiers company in the trenches. The tin shined under the lamp light, silver in color with the initials 'JW' engraved on the bottom. He packed the bowl of his pipe with practiced motions, tamping it down just so.

The match flared as he drew the flame across the tobacco. Sweet smoke curled up as he took a few thoughtful puffs.

"Mind tellin' me why you're fixin' to burn holes through me with those eyes, Mary?"

Mary slapped the newspaper down onto her lap, her anger finally breaking loose like a dam. "You abandoned us, Jesse. You ran off to play soldier and stayed after the war. When Daddy died, Ma wrote you letter after letter, begging you to come home. She needed you. We all needed you." Her voice cracked with pent-up hurt. "And you couldn't be bothered to write back even once?"

Jesse drew quietly on his pipe, letting her words fill the space between them. The little sister who used to follow him around the farm like a shadow now looked at him like a stranger.

"Daddy died, and where were you?" Mary's voice rose, thick with emotion. "Not here. Not helping with the farm. Not comforting Ma. No, you were too busy with your grand adventure in France to care about your family back home." She stood up, hands balled into fists at her sides. "What do you have to say for yourself?"

Jesse tapped his pipe against his palm. "Your anger is justified, Mary. You've carried this farm while I was away, and I'm grateful. But I swear on the Good Lord's Word, I never got any letters. Luke told me about Father today, driving back from the station."

Mary's face went white, her anger faltering. "You... you didn't know?"

"Not one word reached me. If I'd known, I'd have come home immediately."

Mary sank back into her chair, the fight draining from her but the hurt still evident in her eyes. "Jesse, I... I thought..." She pressed her lips together, fighting tears.

Jesse set his pipe aside and moved to kneel beside her chair, just as he used to when she'd skin her knees as a child. "Thank you for keeping our home breathing while I was gone." He reached for her hand, and after a moment's resistance, she let him take it.

Sarah stepped into the sitting room, wiping her hands on her apron. "Lord knows I can't stand seein' my children at odds. It warms my heart to see you two t'gether again."

Jesse shifted in his chair as their mother settled into her rocker. "I need to ask about Father. Who found him?"

"Sheriff Hayes," Sarah said, her hands fidgeting with her apron. "He brought us the news himself."

"What business did he have out near Finley Cave?"

Mary leaned forward. "He told me he was headin' to town to meet someone. Said he'd be back in a day or so. Saddled up his horse and rode off. That was the last time we saw him."

"Did he mention meetin' anyone?"

Mary shook her head. "No, never said."

Jesse drew a deep breath. "And these bank payments? This loan?"

Sarah's head snapped up. "How'd you know bout that?"

"Luke told me today." Jesse caught Mary's expression like a signal flare. "What's troublin' you?"

"What loan?" Mary asked. "What payments?"

Sarah's shoulders slumped. "When the drought hit in '17, we needed money to keep the farm runnin'. It worked for a while, but prohibition changed everythin'. Couldn't sell our corn – the mill stopped buyin', said they was full up. Your Daddy finally found a buyer, some St. Louis outfit, but he stopped dealin' with them months 'fore he…" She paused, collectin' herself.

We had to sell the International truck," Sarah continued. "Now Richmond Bank & Trust – they bought out Springfield Mercantile

Bank. Then they raised our payments – they're threatenin' to take the farm if we can't pay the full balance come next month."

Mary's face hardened. "Why didn't nobody tell me 'bout this?"

"I'm sorry, sweetheart. I thought I was protectin' ya. You had such a hard time after your Daddy's death - I just… I didn't want to worry ya."

Sarah's hands twisted in her lap. "There's somethin' else ya should know, Jesse. Your Daddy… he left everythin' to you. The farm, the equipment, all of it."

Jesse sat back, pipe forgotten in his hand. "That don't make a lick of sense. Why bypass you and Mary?"

"He was set on it," Sarah said. "Changed his will just a month 'fore he passed."

"We weren't even speakin' when I shipped out. It doesn't make sense."

Mary leaned forward. "What 'bout them letters, Ma? Did ya write to Jesse 'bout all this?"

"I sent four, maybe five letters to Koblenz," Sarah said. "And Luke paid good money to send three telegrams from the Frisco Station in Springfield. When we didn't hear nothin' back, we feared the worst."

Jesse's brow furrowed. "Koblenz? I was living there before I left to come home. Those letters should've found me." He set his pipe down, mind racing. "And telegrams always get through - reliable as sunrise. We bet our lives on 'em during the war."

Sarah dabbed at her eyes with her apron. "We was so worried when ya didn't respond. I prayed every night that you was safe."

"When your letter finally came sayin' you was headin' home," Mary added, her voice still tight with lingering hurt, "we thought… well, we thought you'd finally gotten word 'bout Daddy." She looked down at their still-joined hands, then pulled away.

Jesse puffed on his pipe, watching his sister retreat behind her walls again. The sweet tobacco mixed with the evening air as he considered his next words. "Somethin's been naggin' at me. Luke looked mighty unsettled when Hayes walked into the restaurant earlier."

Mary straightened in her chair, her protective instincts flaring. "That's 'cause Luke thinks Hayes had somethin' to do with Daddy's death."

"Mary Walker!" Sarah shot up from her rocker, color draining from her face. "Don't you dare speak such nonsense. Marcus Hayes and your Daddy was like brothers. They loved each other somethin' fierce. Luke's just upset 'bout losin' his uncle, that's all."

Jesse turned to his sister, noting how she set her jaw - the same way she did as a child when she knew something important. "What exactly has our cousin been tellin' you, Mary?"

"Not much." Mary crossed her arms, but Jesse could see the worry in her eyes. "Just that he's got a bad feelin' 'bout Hayes. Said it was mighty suspicious how the sheriff knew exactly where to find Daddy's body. Like he knew right where to look."

Sarah shook her head. "Stop this foolishness right this minute." Her hands trembled as she smoothed her apron.

Jesse drew another thoughtful puff and changed the subject. "I'm ridin' into Springfield tomorrow, see what can be done about these payments."

"No need to go all the way to Springfield," Sarah said, settling back into her rocker. "Richmond opened him a branch in Ozark a while back. Made quite a show of it too – fancy ribbon cuttin' and everythin'."

Jesse rolled the information around in his mind like smoke from his pipe. A new bank branch in Ozark, letters that never arrived, his father's suspicious death, and Luke's strange behavior around Hayes – pieces of a puzzle that didn't quite fit together.

"When exactly did Richmond take over Springfield Mercantile?" Jesse asked, tapping ash from his pipe.

"Couple years back," Sarah replied. "They changed everythin'. New policies, and new payment schedules."

"And that's when the payments started climbin'?"

Mary snorted, her old fire returning. "'Long with half the other farms 'round here. The Hendersons lost their place last month. The Landrys 'fore that." She leaned forward, her voice dropping. "Jesse, somethin' ain't right 'bout any of this."

Jesse's jaw tightened. "Father keep any papers about this loan? Original contract maybe?"

Sarah shook her head. "I ain't been able to find it. The bank oughta have a copy of it."

The crickets outside grew louder as darkness settled over the farm. Jesse caught Mary's eye – despite their years apart, he could still read her thoughts as clearly as when they were children. Too many coincidences.

"We'll sort this out," Jesse said, standing. "Tomorrow, I'm payin' a visit to that bank in town."

Mary grabbed his arm, her earlier anger transformed into concern. "Jesse, be careful. Things ain't like they was 'fore the war. The Ozarks have changed." The grip of her callused fingers spoke of both warning and worry - the touch of a sister who'd already lost too much.

"So have I, little sister." Jesse patted her hand. "So have I."

2

For the Love of Money

Dawn broke over Walker Farm as Jesse made his way down the creaking stairs. The familiar scent of coffee and biscuits drew him to the kitchen, where Sarah stood at the wood stove, her movements precise from years of morning routines.

"Mornin', Mama," Jesse said softly, not wanting to startle her.

She turned, a smile warming her tired face. "You're up early. Some habits don't change, I see." She gestured to the percolator. "Coffee's ready if you want some."

Jesse poured himself a cup, savoring the rich aroma. The kitchen was exactly as he remembered - worn but scrubbed clean, everything in its proper place. The old clock on the wall still ran five minutes fast, just as his father had always kept it.

The screen door squeaked, and Mary entered, already dressed for farm work. She paused briefly at the sight of Jesse, as if remembering all over again that he was really home. Her expression flickered between lingering hurt and cautious hope before settling into something carefully neutral.

"Mornin'," she said, moving to wash her hands at the sink. Jesse noticed fresh scratches on her forearms from working in the fields.

"Been up long?" he asked, trying to bridge the distance between them.

"Since before sun-up. Animals don't feed theirselves." She dried her hands on a towel, then helped Sarah bring breakfast to the table - biscuits, gravy, and eggs from their own hens.

They settled into their chairs, the empty seat at the head of the table a presence none of them could ignore. Sarah bowed her head to say grace, her voice wavering slightly as she thanked the Lord for bringing her son home safe.

"Did ya sleep well?" Sarah asked, passing the biscuits. "I aired out your room best I could, but it's been closed up so long…"

"Just fine, Mama." Jesse spooned gravy over his biscuit. "Though my legs might be too long for that bed now."

"Everything's smaller when ya come back," Mary said quietly, not looking up from her plate. The words carried more weight than just talk about furniture.

Sarah cleared her throat. "Tell us about Paris, Jesse. Your letter mentioned the rebuildin'…"

"Some parts are still pretty torn up," Jesse said carefully, noting how Mary's shoulders tensed at the mention of his time away. "But they're resilient folk. Like us Ozark people - know how to make do and keep goin'."

"Did ya…" Mary started, then seemed to think better of it.

"Go on," Jesse encouraged. "Ask what's on your mind."

She met his eyes then, her own showing a mix of anger and curiosity. "Did ya ever think about us? While you was over there, livin' in them fancy European cities?"

Sarah set down her coffee cup. "Mary, that ain't—"

"No, Mama, it's a fair question," Jesse interrupted gently. "I thought about you every day, Mary. Missed your birthday cakes, Mama's cookin', even your stubborn way of arguin' with me." He tried a small smile. "The French make fine bread, but ain't nobody can touch Mama's biscuits."

"Then why'd ya stay away so long?" Mary's voice cracked slightly. "Even after the fightin' was done?"

Jesse set down his fork, choosing his words carefully. "War changes a man. Had to make sure I was right in the head before comin' home. Didn't want to bring them shadows back to our door." He paused, staring into his coffee cup. "But if I'd known about Father, about the troubles here…"

"Them shadows followed ya home anyway," Mary said quietly. "Your screams had me jumpin' out of bed last night, my heart beatin' fit to burst. Thought someone was dyin' till I realized…" She trailed off, the memory of her panic still fresh.

Sarah's hands trembled slightly as she set down her coffee cup. "I was gonna bring ya some warm milk, like when you was little, but…" Her words drifted, and Jesse knew she'd been afraid to intrude.

"It's alright, Mama." Jesse met their concerned gazes. "No sense pretendin' it ain't there. Some nights are harder than others."

Mary's expression softened, anger giving way to understanding. "I know a tea that might help - learned it from old man Peterson's wife 'fore she passed. Chamomile and lavender, with a touch of honey." She hesitated, then added, "Been makin' it for myself on rough nights, when the worry gets too heavy."

"You ain't alone anymore, son," Sarah said firmly, reaching for both her children's hands. "Whatever shadows followed ya home, we'll face 'em together."

Mary pulled her hand away after a moment, but Jesse noticed she'd shifted her chair slightly closer to his. "I gotta get back to the fields," she said, standing. "Them irrigation ditches won't clear thierselves." She hesitated at the door. "You still take your tea the same way? Two sugars?"

Jesse nodded, surprised she remembered. "Some things don't change."

"Good to know," she said softly. "I'll bring ya that tea tonight. Helps calm the mind before sleep." Then she headed out into the morning sun.

Sarah watched her go, worry lines deepening around her eyes. "Give her time, Jesse. She's had to be so strong for so long."

"I know, Mama." Jesse finished his coffee and stood. "Think I'll head into town, see about them bank papers. Maybe stop by Luke's office after."

"Be careful," Sarah said, and something in her tone made Jesse look back. "Things ain't quite what they seem these days."

Jesse nodded, understanding there was more behind her words than simple motherly concern. "Yes ma'am, I will."

* * *

The morning sun was already burning off the dew when Jesse saddled Baxter. The old bay horse nickered softly, remembering his former master despite the years apart. "Missed you too, old friend," Jesse murmured, running a hand along the horse's neck. Mary had kept him well-groomed, the coat still gleaming like polished copper.

The ride into town gave Jesse time to settle his thoughts. Last night's nightmare still lingered at the edges of his mind, but the familiar sway of the saddle and the steady clip-clop of Baxter's hooves against the packed dirt road helped ground him in the present. The morning sun climbed higher, promising another sweltering July day, and Jesse found himself grateful for the shade of the oak trees lining the road into Ozark.

"Lord above, if it ain't Jesse Walker!" Old Jim Cooper called out from his front porch, rocking chair creaking as he leaned forward. "Bout time you made it back, boy!"

Jesse reined Baxter to a stop, touching the brim of his hat. "Mornin'

Mr. Cooper. Place is lookin' fine."

"Your sister's been supplyin' us with fresh eggs," the old man said, his weathered face creasing into a smile. "That girl's got more spine than most men I know."

"That she does, sir," Jesse agreed, feeling a mix of pride and guilt.

Further down the road, Mrs. Landry waved from her garden, her gray hair peeking out from under a wide-brimmed hat. "Welcome home, Jesse! You tell your mama I'll be by with some preserves soon!"

The town materialized through the summer haze like a mirage. New electric lines stretched between buildings, and prohibition posters plastered storefront windows - progress marching forward even in this corner of Missouri. Jesse dismounted in front of the hitching post near the bank, patting Baxter's neck before securing the reins.

Adjusting his collar and smoothing down his vest, Jesse turned toward Richmond Bank & Trust's polished facade. The familiar faces and warm welcomes had settled something in his chest, but they'd also reminded him of what he was fighting for.

The sunlight cast long shadows through the windows of the bank's Ozark branch as Jesse entered the polished wood lobby. The transition from the dusty street to this carefully curated shrine to wealth made his boots feel suddenly out of place on the gleaming floor. A brass wall calendar near the teller's window caught his eye – July 23rd, 1923. The dog days were here, and with it, the reliable Ozark humidity that seemed to seep through the very walls, despite the bank's attempts at refinement.

The tellers whispered behind their cages, their eyes darting between Jesse and a side office. He recognized Emma Jean Parker behind one of the windows, though she quickly looked away when he caught her eye. They'd gone to school together, once upon a time, before the war changed everything.

"Mr. Walker?" A thin man in wire-rimmed spectacles emerged from the side office, his smile practiced but empty. "I'm Gerald Wilcox. Please, step into my office."

The loan manager's office smelled of leather and polished wood, the air heavy with more than just summer heat. Jesse settled into a chair across from the heavy oak desk, noting how everything in the room seemed designed to project authority and permanence. Even the way Wilcox arranged his desk spoke of a man who enjoyed wielding power over others' futures.

"I understand you're here about the Walker Farm loan," Wilcox said, pulling out a folder with practiced indifference. His movements were too smooth, too rehearsed, like an actor who'd performed the same scene countless times.

"Yes sir. Hopin' we might discuss an extension of terms." Jesse kept his voice steady, though his jaw tightened at Wilcox's dismissive tone. He'd faced German artillery with less tension than he felt in this carefully orchestrated office.

Wilcox adjusted his spectacles, not bothering to look up from the papers. "I'm afraid that won't be possible. Your mother already filed for an extension with our Springfield office. It was denied." He said it with the finality of a man used to crushing hopes.

"Mind tellin' me the outstanding balance?" Jesse watched Wilcox's hands, noting how they twitched slightly at the question.

"The remaining sum is $3,500." Wilcox cleared his throat, glancing briefly at a photograph on his desk. "With mounting interest and late fees, if payment isn't received by the middle of next month, the bank will have no choice but to seize all assets tied to the loan."

Jesse leaned forward, his voice tactfully quiet. "I'd appreciate seein' the appraisal report and loan agreement, if you'd be so kind."

Wilcox's chair squeaked as he shifted backward slightly. "I apologize, Mr. Walker, but we don't keep those documents here." He straightened some papers on his desk, his movements suddenly less precise, almost nervous. "Your father signed the original loan at our Springfield branch, so naturally, all documentation remains there. Bank policy, you understand."

"Seems mighty inconvenient," Jesse observed mildly. "Bank this size, dealin' with local loans, not keepin' proper documentation on hand."

"Bank policy, I'm afraid." Wilcox stood, signaling the end of their meeting. "Now, if you'll excuse me, I have other appointments waiting."

Jesse stood slowly, measuring the man before him. War had taught him to read people, and everything about Wilcox screamed of a man following orders rather than bank policy. The question was: whose orders?

Jesse stepped out of Richmond Bank & Trust into the baking Missouri sun. Emma Jean Parker hurried past him on the sidewalk, clutching bank papers to her chest, barely meeting his gaze. His boots clicked against the wooden sidewalk as he made his way down Ozark's main street.

He pulled a crisp white handkerchief from his back pocket and wiped the sweat from his brow, his eyes scanning the street with the same watchfulness he'd developed in France. The morning's humidity had only gotten worse, causing his hair to stick slightly to his forehead.

The street buzzed with mid-morning activity. Horse-drawn wagons shared the dusty road with automobiles, creating an odd symphony of hooves, wheels, and puttering engines. Shopkeepers propped open doors hoping to catch any hint of breeze, while farmers' wives carried baskets of produce and dry goods between stores. A group of children chased each other past the general store, their bare feet kicking up little clouds of dust.

Luke's law office was just down the street, a converted storefront with fresh paint and polished brass fittings. As Jesse pushed open the door a man with shaggy dark hair and a jagged scar across his right cheek brushed past him, not meeting his eyes as he hurried down the sidewalk.

Inside, a young secretary looked up from her typewriter. "Do you have an appointment?"

"No ma'am, no appointment," Jesse said politely, noting how her fingers nervously played with her pencil. "I'm Luke's cousin, Jesse Walker, just came to have a word."

"Jesse? That you?" Luke's voice carried from the back office. "Come on in!"

Jesse walked past leather-bound law books and framed certificates into Luke's private office. Dark wooden panels lined the walls, and a Persian rug covered the floor. A small statue of Lady Justice stood on a side table next to a leather wingback chair. The blindfolded goddess's right arm stretched skyward, delicate bronze scales dangling from her fingertips, while her left hand gripped a double-edged sword at her side, its tip pointing to the earth.

The office spoke of hard-earned success. Jesse remembered how Luke had worked for this, even as a boy. Before his mother's death, Uncle James and Aunt Sarah had taken him in, raised him alongside Jesse. His grandmother's final gift - a college fund held in trust until he turned eighteen - had given him a chance at education, but Luke had earned every grade, every opportunity that followed.

"Quite the establishment you've made for yourself, cousin." Jesse settled into a chair across from Luke's massive oak desk. "Done well since Saint Louis, I see." He noted how Luke's store-bought suit and gold watch chain seemed at odds with the modest law practice of a small-town lawyer.

Luke smiled, "Can't complain - private practice keeps me busy enough, and the county prosecutor's office even busier since the election last November." His fingers drummed against the desk's polished surface. "Amazing what a few years of law practice and the right connections can do in Christian County. What brings my cousin by?"

Jesse studied his cousin's face, remembering the quiet boy who'd spent hours reading under the oak tree while Jesse and Mary played in the river. Luke had always been different - distant and reserved - though Jesse never quite understood why he'd held himself slightly apart from the family that loved him.

"Mary shared somethin' curious last night." Jesse watched Luke's reaction carefully. "About your thoughts on Hayes and what happened to Father."

The smile vanished from Luke's face. "Jesse, I don't believe this is the best time to—"

"Let's have the straight of it, Luke." Jesse kept his voice steady. "What makes you think Hayes had a hand in it?"

Luke drummed his fingers on the desk, then sighed. His eyes darted to the door before he leaned forward, lowering his voice. "Your father visited me shortly before his passing. He was… well, I'd never seen him in such a state. Said he would 'make Hayes answer for everything' if it was the last thing he did." Luke glanced at the door again. "Then Hayes discovers his body near Finley Cave? Miles from anywhere? The circumstances are… troubling."

Jesse absorbed this silently, noting how Luke's law degree hadn't quite masked his Ozark inflections when under stress. "I'm obliged for your honesty." He stood, mind already working through the implications. "One more thing - might I borrow your automobile? Need to make a trip to Springfield, look into them bank documents about our loan."

"Of course, take it," Luke said, reaching for his keys. "I'll be at the office until six, handling some property matters."

* * *

The Richmond Bank & Trust in Springfield towered over the street corner, its limestone facade casting shadows like prison bars across the sidewalk. Marble columns flanked the entrance, and brass-trimmed revolving doors spun with the steady flow of customers. Inside, the vaulted ceiling loomed overhead, every footstep echoing off marble floors like a judge's gavel.

Jesse's boots clicked against the polished stone as he took his place in line, watching the tellers work behind their cages of polished oak and brass. Each detail of the bank's grandeur seemed designed to make a man feel small. His fingers brushed against the watch in his pocket, each touch fueling a slow-burning anger he kept carefully banked.

When his turn came, a young woman with wire-rimmed glasses looked up expectantly.

"Ma'am, I need to speak with your loan officer, if you please." Jesse's voice carried the same gentle tone he'd use to calm a spooked horse.

"Do you have an appointment, sir?"

"No ma'am, I don't."

"I'm sorry, but the loan officer only sees clients by appointment."

"I understand that, ma'am." Jesse offered a warm smile that reached his eyes. "Might you check if he could spare a moment? I've come from Ozark about an urgent family matter."

She hesitated, then asked, "Who shall I say is inquiring?"

"Jesse Walker."

The name hung in the air like gunsmoke. A round distinguished gentleman passing nearby stopped mid-stride, his tailored Eastern suit and gold watch chain marking him as someone of importance. Despite his refined appearance, his ruddy complexion and burst blood vessels around his nose spoke of expensive habits.

"I shall handle this," he announced, motioning to Jesse with manicured fingers. "Step into my office, Mr. Walker."

Jesse followed him down a carpeted hallway to an office that dripped old money and influence. Oil paintings hung between dark wood panels, and a massive mahogany desk dominated the room like an altar. An elaborately carved humidor sat open, Cuban cigars arranged with precision, their rich tobacco scent mixing with leather and polish. The craftsmanship of the box alone probably cost more than most folks made in a month.

"I am Theodore Richmond," the man said, settling his bulk into a leather chair that creaked in protest. "I own this institution. How may I be of assistance?"

"I'd be obliged to see the appraisal report and loan agreement for the Walker property."

Richmond called through the open door, "Miss Phillips, bring me the Walker farm files." His tone suggested a man used to having his commands obeyed without question.

Turning back to Jesse, he folded his manicured hands on a leather-bound ledger. "What else concerns you?"

"Just returned from service in Europe, sir. Given my father's recent passin', I'm hopin' we might discuss an extension on them payments."

Something shifted in Richmond's expression, like a snake uncoiling. "While I appreciate your service, Mr. Walker, and regret your loss, a contract remains binding."

Jesse leaned forward, every generation of Walker pride in his voice. "Mr. Richmond, I understand business is business. But surely there's room for some Ozark hospitality here. My family's worked that soil since before your bank had its first dollar."

"Hospitality," Richmond's lips curled around the word like it tasted sour, his fingers drumming against the brass corners of his journal. "doesn't satisfy our shareholders, Mr. Walker."

"Give me six months. I'll double the payments to catch up. That land produces the finest corn in Christian County."

Richmond's lips twitched with barely concealed disdain. "The banking industry isn't built on promises and rural sentiments."

"No sir, it's built on people." Jesse kept his voice steady, though his knuckles whitened against his leg. "Folk who work honest and pay their debts. I gave some of my years servin' this country. All I'm askin' is a few months to set things proper."

Richmond selected a cigar from his humidor with deliberate slowness. "Your military service, while commendable," he paused to clip the cap, "has no bearing on this matter. The bank has obligations to consider."

A soft knock preceded Miss Phillips entering with a leather folder. Richmond took it, sliding the documents across the polished desk surface with the air of a man tossing scraps to a dog.

"Here are your documents, Mr. Walker. Review them at your convenience, though I doubt you'll find anything to change our position."

Jesse picked up the folder. The paper felt heavy in his hands – four generations of Walker sweat and blood reduced to numbers in black ink. The original loan from 1917 seemed straightforward enough - $3,500 from Springfield Mercantile at standard terms. But then his eyes caught something that made his pulse quicken - another loan from 1921 he'd never known about. One thousand dollars at an interest rate that would make a back-alley cardsharp blush.

His brow furrowed. Why hadn't his mother or Luke mentioned this loan? He wondered if they even knew about it. His father had always handled the farm's finances, but to keep a debt this size secret...

"This ain't right." Jesse tapped the paper, his finger landing like a hammer strike. "The interest on this second note - it's downright predatory."

Richmond's jowls quivered as he struck a match to his cigar. "The terms were explicitly stated to your father."

"Along with this clause givin' your bank unlimited power to adjust payments whenever you please." Jesse turned to the appraisal with the same precision he'd used reading reconnaissance reports. "And somehow our 350 acres of prime farmland lost half its value between sunset and sunrise?"

"Perhaps farming isn't as viable as it once was." Richmond blew cigar smoke toward the ceiling, each puff punctuating his condescension.

"Or maybe someone's playin' loose with the numbers." Jesse met Richmond's gaze, his eyes as steady as a gunfighter's. "Even us simple hill folk can spot when figures don't add up."

"You dare question my institution's integrity?" Richmond's face deepened from pink to crimson, the burst vessels in his nose practically pulsing. "What could an uneducated farmer possibly know about modern banking?"

"Enough to quote the Federal Reserve Act of 1913 regarding predatory lendin' practices." Jesse said coolly. "Spent my nights in France readin' books, Mr. Richmond. Some of 'em dealt with bankin' law."

Miss Phillips failed to suppress a laugh, cutting it short when Richmond's head snapped toward her like an angry bull's.

The banker's cigar trembled between his fingers as he jabbed them toward the door. "Get out." His voice shook with rage. "You have less than thirty days to pay in full, or the Walker farm becomes bank property."

Jesse stood, tossing the documents back towards Richmond. "You'll have your money, you overstuffed vulture."

Richmond's chair scraped back as he heaved himself up. "Was that a threat, Mr. Walker?"

"No sir," Jesse paused at the door, one hand resting casually on the frame. "That was a fact. Just like them numbers in your books ought to be."

Richmond's cigar snapped between his fingers, tobacco crumbling onto his expensive desk. "How dare—"

"Much obliged for your time," Jesse tipped an imaginary hat as he began to leave the office. "Don't let me keep you from your lunch, Mr.

Richmond - looks like you ain't missed many," he said as he slammed the door behind him.

$$* * *$$

Jesse gripped the steering wheel of Luke's Model T as he drove back toward Ozark, his knuckles white with tension. The numbers from those loan documents kept swimming through his mind. Three thousand five hundred dollars. Less than thirty days. Impossible terms. The same rage that had built in Richmond's office threatened to boil over.

He spotted the old James River Bridge ahead. Just downstream was the deep bend where he and his father used to fish, where he'd learned that sometimes a man needed stillness to think straight. Jesse eased the car onto the weathered planks, then pulled off to the side. He killed the engine, needing silence to sort through the madness of the afternoon.

Stepping out, he walked to the bridge railing. The summer heat pressed down as he stared at the current below, trying to quiet his racing thoughts. A blue heron stalked through the shallows, fishing for its lunch - just like the ones he and his father used to watch from their spot under the sycamores downstream.

His hand found the pocket watch in his vest, thumb running over the worn silver case. What would his father have done? James Walker had been many things - stubborn, hard-headed, fiercely independent - but never a fool with money.

The crack of gunfire shattered his contemplation. Multiple shots echoed off the rocky bluffs, coming from downriver. Jesse's body reacted before his mind could catch up - dropping into a crouch, pulse quickening with familiar adrenaline. In France, gunfire meant running toward trouble, not away from it. Some habits died hard.

Jesse moved through the underbrush with practiced stealth, his boots finding solid ground between roots and fallen branches. The voices grew clearer as he approached - angry shouts mixed with the clatter of metal on metal.

Through a screen of pawpaw leaves, he spotted the scene in a small riverside clearing. Four bodies lay sprawled in the mud, blood darkening their shirts. Three men with rifles worked frantically, loading copper tubing and mason jars into the bed of a battered farm truck. The sweet-sour smell of corn mash hung in the air.

"Get it loaded!" one of them barked. "Someone'll have heard them shots!"

The truck's engine roared to life, tires spinning in mud before finding traction. As the sound of the engine faded into the trees, Jesse moved toward a wounded man who stirred near his position.

"Lie still," Jesse whispered, crouching beside him and pulling out his handkerchief. Blood seeped through the cloth as he pressed it against the chest wound - too much blood. The man grabbed Jesse's sleeve, eyes wide with panic.

"Finley River Gang," the man wheezed. "Bunch of thieves..." His grip went slack, eyes fixing on nothing.

Behind a screen of river cane stood a professional still setup with multiple cookers and fermentation barrels sunk into the ground. The gang had known exactly what they were after.

He couldn't be here when people came to investigate the gunfire. With bank troubles already hanging over his head, being found at the scene of a shootout would only make things worse. Jesse moved fast through the trees, keeping low. He had to get back to that Model T and clear out before anyone else showed up.

* * *

Jesse struck a match and lit the brass lantern on his father's roll-top desk, the warm glow filling his old study in the sitting room. He settled into the creaky leather chair, his hands trembling slightly as he packed his pipe. Today's violence had stirred up memories he'd thought long buried - the wet gurgle of a dying man's breath, the desperate grip of fingers clawing at his shirt, the spreading dark stain that no amount of pressure could stop. Not since the trenches in France had he watched life drain from a man's eyes.

He glanced down at his hands. He'd scrubbed them raw at the pump outside, but a faint rust-colored stain still lingered beneath one fingernail. Jesse shook his head, forcing the ghosts back into their box. He lit his pipe with practiced motions, letting the sweet smoke ground him in the present, then began pulling open drawers, rifling through stacks of yellowed papers.

The desk still smelled of his father's pipe tobacco - different blend than Jesse's Bull Durham, earthier somehow. He found himself hesitating over each document, studying his father's precise handwriting.

Mary's soft footsteps approached from the hallway. "Any luck at the bank today?"

Jesse shook his head, not looking up from the papers. "They won't budge on the extension. Richmond made it clear like Marley's ghost."

"What are we going to do?" Mary twisted her hands in her apron. "We can't lose the farm, Jesse. This land is all we have."

"I'll think of somethin'." He pulled open another drawer, scanning through more documents. "Tell me, did Father mention any peculiar dealings before he passed? Any new business ventures?"

Mary leaned against the wall. "Nothing specific. Though he'd started riding out to the holler at the end of the property most afternoons. Never said why - just that he had 'things to tend to.' Went on for weeks before..." She trailed off.

Jesse's pipe paused halfway to his mouth. The holler - a deep, wooded valley at the edge of their land. As kids, they'd been strictly forbidden from playing there. "The holler, you say?"

"Mhmm. Sometimes he wouldn't come back 'til after dark. Ma'd worry herself sick, but you know how Daddy was once he got somethin' in his head."

Jesse nodded slowly, already planning to investigate the spot at first light. Something about that detail nagged at him, like a splinter under the skin.

3

Cave of Secrets

The summer morning bore down on Jesse as he guided Baxter through the familiar paths of Walker Farm. The horse's hooves kicked up dust from the dry earth as they made their way southeast, past fields where corn stalks swayed in the morning breeze.

The terrain grew rougher as they approached the holler, the fertile farmland giving way to rocky hills and dense woods. Jesse's mind drifted to memories of this place as a child, particularly that day they called "The Great Blue Norther."

The sky had turned an eerie shade of green-black, and the wind howled like a freight train. His mother had grabbed him by the arm, her fingers digging into his sleeve as his father rushed them all toward the cave. Jesse remembered how his heart had pounded in his chest, how the wind had nearly knocked him off his feet.

Inside the cave, they'd huddled together, listening to the storm rage outside. His father had lit a lantern, the flickering light casting strange shadows on the limestone walls. The sound of the wind echoed through the cave's mouth like some ancient beast's roar.

Even now, after facing artillery barrages in France, the thought of those Ozark storms made Jesse's skin crawl. He'd seen what tornadoes could do - barns splintered like matchsticks, entire crops flattened, lives changed in an instant. But the night storms were the worst. In the pitch black, you couldn't see them coming. Just the roar, and then… nothing.

Baxter carefully made his way through the hills and holler coming to a stop in front of the cave's mouth. Jesse dismounted, his boots crunching on gravel. Moss-covered rocks flanked the entrance, wide enough for a man to pass without ducking. The cave's dark maw seemed to breathe cool air against his face.

Jesse ran his hand along the rough stone wall, remembering how his father had taught him to navigate these passages. Some led nowhere, dead-ending in tight squeezes or rubble. Others… well, even after all these years, Jesse wasn't sure where they all went. But there was one main chamber he knew well, a cathedral-like space where the ceiling opened up high enough that you couldn't see it with a lantern's light.

If his father had been coming out here those final weeks, that chamber would be the place to start looking. Jesse tied Baxter's reins to a young dogwood tree near the entrance, giving the horse enough slack to graze on the sparse highland grass.

From the saddle holster, he pulled his father's old Henry Repeater. The rifle's wooden stock was smooth from years of use, its brass receiver dulled by time but still solid. Jesse worked the lever action, the familiar click-clack echoing off the cave walls. He grabbed the lantern hanging from his saddle horn, struck a match, and lit it. With rifle in one hand and lantern in the other, Jesse stepped into the cave's cool darkness.

The lantern's light danced upon the cave walls, each flicker bringing life to the limestone formations. Water dripped somewhere in the darkness, each drop echoing through the passages like nature's metronome. The musty scent of wet earth and mineral-rich stone filled Jesse's nostrils, mixed with the occasional whiff of bat guano.

The passage widened in places, narrowed in others. Jesse ducked beneath low-hanging stalactites, their surfaces slick and cold. His boots scraped against the uneven ground, the sound bouncing off the walls. Here and there, patches of cave moss caught the lantern light, glowing an ethereal green.

At a junction where the passage split three ways, Jesse paused. Fresh tracks marked the cave floor - boot prints pressed into mud, still wet enough to catch the light. They led left, toward the main chamber. Jesse had explored that vast space countless times as a boy, but something felt different now.

He dialed down the lantern's flame until it barely lit the ground before him. The familiar weight of the Henry rifle steadied his hands as he followed the tracks. With each step deeper into the passage, an acrid smell grew stronger - sharp and chemical, nothing like the cave's natural odors.

The passage curved slightly, and ahead, flickering light spilled from the entrance to the main chamber. It pulsed against the walls, casting moving shadows that had nothing to do with Jesse's lantern.

Jesse set his lantern down and raised his rifle, edging toward where the chamber met the passageway. He peered around the corner into the vast space beyond. Two massive copper stills stood center of the chamber, their smooth surfaces gleaming in the lamplight. Steam hissed from copper coils that snaked down into wooden barrels. The larger still stood nearly eight feet tall, its pot belly swollen like a pregnant sow. The smaller one looked newer, its metal still bright and untarnished.

An older man worked between them, adjusting valves and checking temperatures. His ancient overalls were patched in a dozen places, and his handmade boots scraped against the stone floor as he shuffled around, singing in a thick Ozark drawl:

"Sweet cawn whiskey, cleah as glass,
Makes a preachuh dance in th' grass,
Rev'nuers come a-sniffin' 'round,

But they ain't gonna find whut cain't be found!"

Jesse moved silently forward, his military training taking over as he placed each foot carefully on the rocky ground. When he was five feet from the old moonshiner, he cocked his Henry. The sharp click echoed through the chamber.

The old man froze mid-verse, then spoke slowly turning around: "Well shoot fahr, if'n yer gonna keel me, least lemme finish this here batch. Be a turrible waste of good cawn otherwise."

Jesse kept the rifle trained on the old man. "Mind tellin' me who you are and why you're runnin' shine on Walker land?"

The old man turned slowly, hands raised, revealing a weathered face mapped with deep wrinkles and missing two fingers on his left hand. "Name's Bill Thompson, an' I take 'fense to ya callin' this just 'shine. This here's th' finest moonshine an' whiskey in all th' Ozarks. Yer daddy knew that better'n most."

My father wouldn't...He wouldn't be mixed up in somethin' illegal like this."

Bill's laugh echoed off the cave walls. "His idee, matter of fact! You must be Jesse. James talked 'bout you plenty, said you'd come home someday." He shifted his weight, and Jesse adjusted his aim. "Easy now, boy. Yer daddy left sumthin' fer ya."

"Don't move," Jesse warned, tracking Bill with the rifle.

"Settle yerself down. I'm just a-fetchin' a letter." Bill shuffled over to a crude living space carved into the cave wall - a rickety desk and narrow bed suggesting long-term residence. He rummaged through a drawer, tossing aside dried corn kernels onto the desk. "Ah, here we go."

He extracted an envelope with 'Jesse' written in familiar handwriting - his father's penmanship. Bill held it out carefully, then backed away to sit on his bed. Uncorking a jug of clear liquid, he took a long pull.

"Read it," Bill said, wiping his mouth with his sleeve. "Yer daddy had his reasons."

Jesse moved closer to the lantern, unfolding the letter with careful hands. The paper was worn but clean, his father's distinctive handwriting flowing across the page. Dated just a week before his death:

"Dear Jesse,

I need to ask your forgiveness, son - not just for what I'm about to tell you, but for how I acted when you left. My pride was hurt something fierce when you went off to war. That's a father's foolishness for you. Come to understand it better now, why you had to go see the world for yourself.

This prohibition's got everything twisted up wrong. Corn prices fell through the floor, mills barely buying. Railroad rates and tariffs eating what little profit we had. Got backed into taking another loan from Richmond Bank. Should've known better - interest is crushing us now.

Met a fellow named Parsons outside the bank in Springfield. Said he'd pay good money for steady grain supply - double what mills were paying. Peculiar thing was, his trucks would come to us, twice a month like clockwork. Should've questioned that more. What legitimate business doesn't want you delivering to them?

Year ago, found old Bill Thompson living in our cave. Was fixing to run him off at first, but something about that old coot... He got me thinking straight about things. That much grain we were selling to Parsons - ain't but one thing it could be used for in these times, and it sure wasn't bread. Made me sick knowing what we were really feeding.

Had to stop selling to Parsons after that, but then Richmond Bank raised our payments. Bill offered a way out - said he knew how to keep the farm, but it'd mean walking a crooked path. Lord forgive me, Jesse, but I chose the farm. Chose family.

These past months, them Finley River Boys been showing their true colors. Mean bunch of moonshiners running most of the liquor trade from Christian County clear down to Arkansas. They're taking over territory, clearing out anyone who won't fall in line. Getting closer every day. That's why I'm writing this - in case things go wrong.

Bill will explain everything - he's crazy as a betsy bug, but there ain't a soul in these hills knows more about these matters. Watch over Mary - she's got my stubborn streak and then some. And Jesse... take care of your mother. Sarah's the best thing that ever happened to me.

God keep you, son.

-Pa

March 12, 1923"

Jesse slid to the ground, his back against the rocky chamber, tears fell from his eyes. He hadn't cried like this, not since in the trenches in France. He had always thought his dad was mad at him and it ate him up knowing he never got to tell his father sorry. But in the end, his father did the unsuspected, he asked for Jesse's forgiveness. He never expected that. Jesse wiped the tears from his eyes.

"Don't take on so, boy." Bill shuffled over and patted Jesse's shoulder with his maimed hand. "Yer daddy loved ya sumthin' fierce. Why, one time he got so worked up talkin' 'bout you winnin' them battles in France, he knocked over mah best batch. Had ta sleep outside three days on 'count of th' fumes." Bill scratched his head. "Course, mighta been why I saw them dancin' purple chickens that week. Never could quite figger that part out."

Jesse took a deep breath, steadying himself. "So, Bill, reckon your tale rings true. You and my father were partners in this illegal venture?"

"Ain't nuthin' illegal 'bout it!" Bill spat on the cave floor. "Guvmint's dumber'n a box a rocks, thinkin' they can take mah precious whiskey 'way from folks. Might as well try stoppin' th' sun from risin'.'"

"Bill, do you know who put my father in the ground?"

Bill shook his head, his weathered face growing serious. "James never told me things like that. Truth is, I hardly leave this cave 'cept maybe once't or twice't every couple weeks. Cave suits me fine - fewer people means fewer problems."

"Next big shipment of shine'll be ready in a few weeks," Bill continued, checking one of the copper coils. "Got us a contact up in Kansas City a-waitin'."

"I don't know about steppin' into unlawful waters—"

"Bit late fer that, ain't it?" Bill shuffled back to his desk. "This here's th' only thing gonna save yer farm." He pulled open another drawer and extracted an envelope. "Yer daddy's share from our last delivery."

Jesse opened it, his eyes widening at the stack of bills inside. "There must be near two thousand dollars here."

"Yep," Bill cackled. "An' that's just from one delivery. Why, last time I saw a man's eyes bug out like that, he'd just kissed mah cousin Mabel's pet mule!"

"How many gallons did you sell?"

"Eighty gallons that run. Next delivery's near 'bout hundred fifty gallons - means more money." Bill tapped the larger still. "I don't keep much from th' sale, just enough. All I need's mah batch from th' still, count it as partial payment. Yer daddy let me live here free, seein' as I know how ta run these beauties."

Jesse ran a hand through his hair, overwhelmed. "Need to think on this a spell."

"Don't think too long," Bill warned. "Plans need makin'."

* * *

Jesse sat on the porch, the old rocker creaking beneath him as he packed fresh tobacco into his pipe. The ritual calmed him - tamping down the leaves, striking the match, drawing that first slow pull. Nearly two thousand dollars lay hidden upstairs, enough to cover half their debt. But Richmond wanted it all, and he wanted it soon.

What would he tell Mary and his mother about the money? He could claim army savings, they'd believe that. But the lie stuck in his throat like bitter smoke.

He puffed thoughtfully, watching the sun sink toward the treeline. All his life he'd believed in justice, in right and wrong. The army had only strengthened that - rules and order keeping chaos at bay. Now here he was, contemplating running shine just like his father.

His father. The thought twisted in his gut. James Walker had always preached honest work and following the law. What had driven him to break his own principles? Jesse could almost hear his father's voice: "Sometimes a man's gotta choose 'tween what's legal and what's right."

But was it right? Or just convenient? He'd seen enough death in France to know how quickly violence followed illegal trades. Yet sitting idle while Richmond stole their land felt like its own kind of wrong.

The sweet-scented pipe smoke drifted up, mingling with the evening chorus of cicadas. Their steady drone was nothing like the shells that still echoed in his dreams sometimes. After the war and wandering France's grand cities, the simple peace of an Ozark sunset felt like a blessing. Home was worth fighting for - but at what cost?

4

A Doughboy In Need

The heat pressed down like a heavy blanket as Jesse entered the sheriff's office. He removed his flat cap, drawing a handkerchief across his brow while Deputy Cole jerked up from his paperwork, knocking over an ink bottle. His hands shook slightly as he cleaned up the spill.

"What can I do fer ya today, Jesse?" Cole's voice wavered.

"Need to see the sheriff. Come to pick up some items from him."

Cole's adam's apple bobbed as he swallowed. "Oh... them things. Right." He shuffled some papers on his desk, not meeting Jesse's eyes. "The sheriff'll be with ya in a minute. Been... been expectin' you'd come by."

A drunken melody drifted from the cells - familiar words that transported Jesse straight back to the muddy trenches of France.

"Over there, over there... Send the word, send the word over there..." The voice was rough but carried the tune well enough. "That the Yanks are coming, the Yanks are coming... The drums rum-tumming everywhere..."

Jesse walked to the cells, memories of battlefield campfires and nervous soldiers singing to keep their spirits up flooding back. He joined in, his clear voice mixing with the drunk's: "So prepare, say a prayer… Send the word, send the word to beware… We'll be over, we're coming over… And we won't come back till it's over, over there!"

Laughter erupted from the cell as the disheveled man stumbled to his feet, gripping the iron bars for balance. His eyes were bloodshot but held a familiar haunted look Jesse knew too well.

Jesse studied the man through the bars, seeing a reflection of his own struggles. Every man who'd come back carried the war differently - some drowned it in whiskey, others in work. Jesse had chosen the latter, but there were still nights when the thunder sounded too much like artillery, when the faces of fallen friends visited his dreams.

"Fellow doughboy?" Jesse asked.

The man attempted a salute, nearly toppling over in the process. "35th Division," he slurred proudly. "Corporal, Company B."

"35th? No kidding? So was I! Sergeant, Company D. Were you at Meuse-Argonne?"

"Yeah…" the man's expression darkened. "Some nights I don't leave there."

"Name's Tom Miller," he added after a moment.

"Prohibition ain't exactly winnin' this war neither, is it Tom?"

Miller laughed, casting an exaggerated glance at the deputy. "There's ways to get a good drink. I'd tell ya, but the law's listenin'."

The deputy rolled his eyes, returning to his paperwork.

"Bit early to be chasin' them shadows, ain't it?" Jesse asked gently.

"Only way not to see their faces," Miller muttered, his brief mirth fading.

Jesse nodded slowly, the ghosts of the Argonne flickering at the edges of his own memory. Siegfried Sassoon's words echoed in his mind - *you smug-faced crowds with kindled eye, who cheer when soldier lads march by, sneak home and pray you'll never know the hell where youth and laughter go.* He'd found his way back through those verses, through wandering the healing fields of France where wildflowers now bloomed in old shell craters. Watching the land rebuild from the ashes of war had shown him his own mind could do the same. He pushed the poetry aside and said softly, "Hold fast, Tom. War's over, but some battles we still gotta fight."

Looking at Miller, Jesse saw a mirror of what could have been - what still might be if he hadn't stayed in Europe, if he hadn't lost himself in books and found himself in watching broken countries slowly mend.

Sheriff Hayes's door creaked open. "Well, look who's here - come on in, son."

The office smelled of leather a gun oil. A gun rack hung behind the sheriff's desk, while wanted posters and county notices covered the walls. Sunlight streamed through venetian blinds, casting striped shadows across the wooden floor.

Hayes settled into his chair, the leather creaking beneath as he sat. "What can your old friend do for ya today?"

"Come to collect my father's effects," Jesse said. "The ones he had when you found him."

"Ah." Hayes nodded slowly."Been wonderin' when somebody'd come collect those. Was fixin' to bring 'em out to your mama myself one of these days."

He pushed himself up from his chair and walked to a small closet in the corner. The hinges protested as he opened it, reaching inside to pull out a weathered cardboard box. His boots scuffed against the floor as he returned to his desk, setting the box down and sliding it across the scarred wood toward Jesse.

"Here ya go, son."

Jesse lifted the lid off the cardboard box. Inside lay his father's everyday items - a worn leather wallet, a pocket knife with a bone handle, his father's old brass pocket watch that hadn't worked in years. Nothing remarkable. Nothing that spoke to why he'd been out there that day.

"Mind if I ask you somethin', Sheriff?"

"What's on your mind, Jesse?" Hayes leaned back, his chair groaning.

"What business did my father have out by Finley Cave?"

"Lord, son, wish I knew." Hayes's fingers drummed against his desk like distant thunder. "Wasn't his usual stompin' grounds, that's certain."

"How'd you manage to locate him in all that wilderness? That's a mighty precise find in rough country."

"Got a call here at the office," Hayes's eyes drifted past Jesse's shoulder, as if he was searching old memories. "Anonymous tip. Never did catch who made it. Been tryin' to track down whoever called - figure they might know somethin' about what happened. Could've even had a hand in it themselves."

Jesse watched Hayes's face. The sheriff's usual steady gaze kept shifting away.

"One more thing - Luke mentioned there was some discord between you and my father before his passin'."

Hayes shook his head. "Don't recollect nothin' like that. Luke must be mistaken." His eyes narrowed slightly. "What makes ya ask about that?"

"Just tryin' to piece together his final days." Jesse kept his voice neutral, though doubt gnawed at him. Something in Hayes's manner felt off, rehearsed almost.

Through the open door, Miller had started humming another tune - something soft and sad from the trenches. Jesse thought of the look in the man's eyes, that familiar darkness. He'd been lucky, finding his way back through pain. Some men weren't so fortunate. Maybe he could do something about that, at least for one lost soldier.

Jesse shifted in his chair, deciding to change course. "Tell me 'bout Tom Miller. Known him long?"

"Poor boy mostly drifts 'tween Christian and Greene counties. Family farm got took by the bank while he was servin' overseas - lost his folks to that awful Spanish Flu 'fore he made it back." Hayes shook his head. "Been wanderin' ever since. Folks say he's right handy with engines and such."

"What landed him in your care?"

"Found him carryin' on in front of the mercantile, drunk as a coon in a wine barrel. Can't let that slide with them federal boys watchin' us so close." Hayes rubbed his temple. "He'll dry out a few days less somebody pays his fine. Though Lord knows, give him steady work, and he'd likely drink away every penny of it."

"What's he owe?"

"One dollar." Hayes snorted. "Sure wish he'd tell me where he keeps gettin' the shine. Them federal boys keep pushin' us to crack down harder. This prohibition business is a pain in my ass."

"Can't argue with that." Jesse reached for his billfold and pulled out a dollar. He held the bill out to Hayes. "Here. Set him loose."

Hayes took the money with a slow nod. "That's mighty kind of you, Jesse. Most folks these days wouldn't spare two cents for a drunk soldier."

Jesse tucked the cardboard box under his arm and rose from his chair. "Much obliged for keepin' these safe, Sheriff. Mama'll find comfort in having them back."

"Your daddy was proud of you, Jesse. Even if he wasn't one to show it proper." Hayes stood, adjusting his gun belt. "Lord knows that man could be stubborn as a Missouri mule, but he loved his family somethin' fierce."

"About his case…" Jesse paused at the door. "If anything new comes to light, or that anonymous caller shows themselves, I'd be grateful to know."

Hayes's weathered face softened. "Course I will, son. You're practically family." He clapped Jesse's shoulder. "Been keepin' my ear to the ground, askin' around quiet-like. Moment I learn anythin' solid, you'll be the first to know."

Jesse studied the sheriff's face one last time, searching for any hint of deception behind those familiar features. But Hayes's expression remained open, concerned - exactly what you'd expect from a family friend. Maybe Luke's suspicions were wrong. Or maybe Hayes was a better actor than Jesse gave him credit for.

* * *

Jesse sat on the worn wooden bench outside the sheriff's office, his father's belongings tucked safely in the cardboard box beside him. The summer heat had softened slightly as clouds drifted across the sun. The door creaked open and Tom Miller stepped out, squinting against the daylight. His shoulders were straighter now, the worst of the drink wearing off.

"Heard ya paid my fine," Tom said, working his jaw. "I don't take charity from nobody."

Jesse nodded, studying the man's weathered face. "How about earnin' it instead?"

"What kind of work?" Tom's bloodshot eyes held a glimmer of interest.

"Ever worked soil before?"

A ghost of a smile crossed Tom's face. "Half my life, before..." He didn't finish the sentence, but Jesse understood. Before the war changed everything.

"Good. Walker Farm could use another set of hands for a spell. Room and board provided - that'll square the debt proper."

Tom considered this, running a hand through his unkempt hair. His military bearing showed through now that he was sobering up - the way he squared his shoulders, how he assessed Jesse with careful eyes.

"Reckon that's fair enough." Tom extended his hand. "And… thank ya. For gettin' me outta there."

Jesse clasped his hand, feeling the familiar calluses of a working man. They shook firmly, sealing the agreement.

* * *

Jesse sat in the farmhouse kitchen, enduring Mary's frustrated pacing. She'd been going on for ten minutes about his decision to invite Tom Miller to the farm.

"A drunk? Ya invited a drunk to stay with us?" Mary's hands landed on her hips. "Have ya lost your mind?"

"He ain't just some wanderin' drunk, Mary. He's a fellow doughboy who needs a helpin' hand." Jesse tamped tobacco into his pipe. "Fought the same blood-soaked ground I did in France. Plus the man knows his way 'round a farm."

Mary threw her hands up. "Oh, that makes it all better! A drunk who knows how to farm!"

"That's enough, Mary." Sarah's calm voice cut through the tension as she dried dishes. "We sure could use the help, 'specially while Jesse figures out how to save the farm." She paused, moving to the front window. "Lord have mercy…"

"What is it, Mother?" Jesse asked.

Sarah peered down the long driveway. "That must be him comin' up now."

Mary couldn't help herself - she moved to the window, her protest dying on her lips as she watched the tall figure making his way up the path. "Well," she managed, trying to keep her voice stern despite the flush creeping up her neck. "Least he walks straight enough."

"Mhmm," Sarah hummed knowingly, hiding a smile.

"I best go… wash up 'fore supper," Mary announced suddenly. "Been workin' in the garden all day."

"Garden work didn't seem to bother ya none five minutes ago," Sarah observed mildly.

"Well, it bothers me now," Mary retorted, heading for the washroom. She paused in the doorway, adding with forced irritation, "And don't think this means I approve of Jesse bringin' home strays."

Jesse caught his mother's eye as Mary disappeared, both of them sharing a knowing look at his sister's transparent excuse.

"Tom," Jesse called from the porch. "Welcome to Walker Farm. You're just in time for supper."

Tom ducked his head in thanks as he stepped inside, removing his worn cap. Sandy brown hair, in need of a trim, fell across his forehead. Jesse noticed Mary watching their new farmhand's entrance from the corner of her eye, despite her determined focus on setting the table. Her hands fumbled slightly with a fork when Tom absently pushed that unruly hair back from his face.

Jesse watched Tom settle at their supper table, noting how his sister was working mighty hard to look anywhere but at their new farmhand. Of course, that didn't stop Mary from stealing glances when she thought nobody was watching - her eyes lingering on his strong jawline before she'd catch herself and return to glaring at her empty plate.

Sarah moved around the table with practiced grace, ladling generous portions of ham and beans into each bowl. When she reached Tom, he straightened his back like he was back in formation.

"Thank you kindly, Mrs. Walker." Tom's voice was soft but clear, his manners showing through despite his worn appearance.

Sarah took her seat at the head of the table, folding her hands. "Let us bow our heads and thank the Lord for this bounty."

They all bowed their heads as Sarah led the blessing, though Jesse noticed Mary peeking through her lashes at Tom. When the collective "Amen" finished, Jesse grabbed the bowl of fresh cornbread from the center of the table.

He passed pieces around, watching Tom's hands shake slightly as he accepted his portion. Jesse crumbled his own cornbread into his bowl of ham and beans, the familiar motion bringing back memories of countless family meals.

Tom took a cautious bite, then his eyes widened. "Mrs. Walker. This is… this is somethin' else. Ain't had cookin' like this since 'fore the war, reminds me of my Mama's table."

Sarah's face softened at the compliment. "Why thank ya, Tom. You're welcome to seconds once ya finish that bowl."

Mary, who had been pushing her beans around with her spoon, finally spoke up. "So Tom," she said, her tone trying to sound more accusatory than curious, "was ya in the same division as Jesse? Did ya fight at Saint-Mihiel too?"

Tom's fingers tightened around his spoon, his knuckles whitening. A distant look crossed his face as he stared into his bowl.

Jesse cleared his throat. "Say Tom, how do ya feel about puttin' your hand to work come mornin'? Reckon you'll be steady enough?"

Mary flushed at Jesse's stern look, her expression flickering between embarrassment and annoyance. She stabbed at her beans with renewed focus, though Jesse caught her casting a concerned glance at Tom's troubled face.

"We're mighty grateful for the help," Sarah said, smoothly filling the awkward silence. "Lord knows there's plenty needin' done 'round here."

Tom's shoulders relaxed slightly. "It's me who should be grateful, ma'am. Jesse here done me a real favor." He studied his plate, cheeks flushing. "Least I can do is help out where I'm needed. Tomorrow's fine by me."

Sarah sighed, stirring her beans. "With the bank breathin' down our necks, we need all the hands we can get."

"The bank?" Tom looked up, concern etching his features. "I didn't know…"

"We'll sort that out," Jesse said firmly, not wanting to burden their guest with their troubles.

Mary, who had been watching Tom's genuine concern with something close to approval, caught herself and tried to sound stern. "Well, Mr. Miller, ya best get your beauty rest tonight. Tomorrow I'm gonna work ya harder than any drill sergeant ever did." Despite her attempt at severity, there was a hint of playfulness in her voice she couldn't quite hide.

A genuine smile broke across Tom's weathered face. "Yes ma'am. Lookin' forward to it."

* * *

A full moon hung over the Walker farm as a chorus of frogs filled the summer night with their endless song. A sharp scream cut through the peaceful darkness, jolting Mary from her sleep. She sat bolt upright, her heart hammering against her ribs.

Without hesitation, she grabbed her daddy's old 12-gauge from beside her bed and slipped her feet into her work boots, not bothering to lace them. Her white cotton nightgown billowed around her legs as she rushed down the stairs and out into the muggy night air.

The screaming had come from the direction of the barn. Mary's boots kicked up dust as she ran across the yard, the shotgun steady in her grip. The guest quarters attached to the barn had a single light burning behind its curtained window.

"Tom?" Mary called out, pounding on the wooden door with her free hand. "Tom, ya alright in there?"

She heard movement inside, then Tom's voice, thick with sleep and something else. "I'm… I'm okay. Just give me a minute."

The door creaked open, revealing Tom in his undershirt and trousers, his hair disheveled and face sheened with sweat. His eyes were wild, like those of a spooked horse.

"I'm sorry, Miss Mary," he stammered, running a trembling hand through his hair. "Didn't mean to wake nobody. Sometimes I… sometimes I get them bad dreams is all."

Mary lowered the shotgun, her concern evident in her face. "Can I come in?"

Tom hesitated for a moment, then stepped aside. "Course ya can, miss. Though I ain't exactly fixed up for company."

Mary was suddenly very aware of her own nightgown, and even more aware of Tom's undershirt clinging to his broad shoulders. She gripped the shotgun tighter, grateful for something to do with her hands. "I'll… I'll fetch us some tea. Helps with the nerves."

"Ya don't have to-" Tom started, but Mary was already turning toward the house.

"Won't be but a minute," she called over her shoulder, trying to keep her voice steady. Truth was, she needed a moment to collect herself.

When she returned with her mother's kettle and cups, wearing a light shawl over her nightgown, Tom sat on the edge of his bed, hands still trembling. Mary pulled the room's only chair close to the small table, pointedly avoiding looking at how Tom's undershirt stretched across his chest as he leaned forward.

"Here," she handed him a cup of steaming tea, careful not to let their fingers brush. "This'll settle them nerves."

Tom wrapped his fingers around the warm cup, staring down into the dark liquid. "I'm mighty sorry 'bout all this, Miss Mary. A grown man shouldn't be-"

"Ain't nothin' to be ashamed of," Mary cut him off gently, focusing on pouring her own tea to distract herself from the way his hair fell across his forehead. "Even Jesse gets his share of nightmares since comin' home. War changes a man, my daddy used to say."

Tom took a careful sip. "Did I wake your brother? Or your ma?"

"Jesse takes this same tea most nights," Mary said, smoothing her nightgown. "Before the war, that boy could sleep through anythin'. Now..." She shook her head. "But Ma? She sleeps like the dead. Wouldn't hear a tornado if it carried the house away."

She studied the steam rising from her cup. "Ya know, since daddy passed this spring, I've been gettin' these terrible dreams myself. Not like your war dreams, mind you, but..." Mary paused, surprised at herself for sharing this. "I wake up certain I heard him callin' for help. Still ain't used to him bein' gone, truth be told."

Tom looked up at her then, really looked at her, and Mary felt her cheeks warm. "Must be hard," he said softly. "Takin' on all this."

"Weren't no other choice," Mary shrugged, trying to sound matter-of-fact. "Jesse was away in France, and somebody had to help Ma keep things runnin'. Had to learn more about farm work these past few months than I ever thought I would. Daddy always said I was too headstrong for my own good - guess that came in handy after all."

"Thank ya for the tea, Miss Mary. And for... understandin'." Tom's eyes held a respect that made Mary's heart flutter traitorously.

Tom shifted uncomfortably, opened his mouth to speak, then looked away, color rising in his cheeks.

"What is it?" Mary asked.

"I was wonderin'..." Tom cleared his throat. "Would ya...would ya mind sittin' in that chair for a spell? Just till I fall asleep? I'd feel better knowin' someone was..." He trailed off, embarrassed.

Mary's face softened. "Course I will."

5

The Devil's Share

The pungent smell of fermenting mash filled the cave chamber as Bill stirred another batch in the copper still. The huge metal vessel, scarred and dented from years of use, sat atop a carefully controlled fire pit. A complex network of copper tubing snaked from the still's cap into cooling barrels filled with spring water. Jesse watched from his perch on an old wooden crate, pipe smoke curling around his head like morning fog over the Finley River.

"Wal' boy, ye been powerful quiet these past few days," Bill said, wiping his brow with a sleeve that looked older than the Civil War itself. "Time's a'tickin'. Made up yer mind yit 'bout our arrangement?"

Jesse pulled the pipe from his mouth, studying the glowing ember. The sweet cherry tobacco taste lingered as he considered his response. Something about old Bill reminded him of his father - maybe it was the way the old-timer handled the still with the same care Jesse's father had shown his prized hunting rifle, or how he'd mutter to himself while working, just like father used to do in the fields.

"Ya knew my father well?" Jesse asked, watching Bill test the mash with practiced movements.

"Only knowed him this past year or so," Bill nodded, his remaining fingers adjusting the fire beneath the still with surprising precision. "But Lord, if'n we didn't become thick as thieves right quick. Weren't no better man to have at yer back." He paused, testing the temperature. "He talked 'bout you often, ya know. Proud as could be of his soldier boy."

Jesse studied the old moonshiner's face, seeing the genuine grief there. "Never knew he was involved in…" He gestured at the still.

"Shore was. Man had principles 'bout fair play. When them banks started squeezin' folks dry, well…" Bill grinned, his few remaining teeth gleaming in the lantern light. "He reckoned if'n they was gonna try'n take his land, he'd do whatever it took to keep that farm in Walker hands. Weren't nothin' more important to yer pa than protectin' his family."

Jesse sat back down, the weight of his father's choices still heavy on his mind. The sweet smell of corn mash mixing with mineral-rich cave air seemed to carry echoes of his presence. "Truth is, I don't see another path to satisfy the bank's appetite."

"That's whut yer daddy said too." Bill tested the temperature of the still with his maimed hand. "Reckon ye'll take to it jist like he did."

"I'll help until we square things with Richmond's vultures," Jesse said firmly from his perch on the crate. "After that, I'm done with this particular venture."

Bill cackled, the sound echoing off the cave walls like a murder of crows taking flight. "That's whut ye say fer now. Once ye git yerself a taste of this life, tain't no goin' back. Speakin' of which, got us a right fine opportunity come tomorrow night."

"What kind of opportunity?" Jesse's hand unconsciously moved to touch the revolver at his hip, a habit from his infantry days.

"Local speakeasy down-river ways, The Jumpin' Frog. They's wantin' fifty gallon. Offerin' three hunnerd dollars." Bill's eyes twinkled with the prospect of the deal.

Jesse frowned, his war-weathered face creasing. "That all? Thought this particular enterprise paid better."

"Prices change a'pendin' on where yer sellin'," Bill explained, carefully checking the copper tubing connections. "Local folk ain't got them Kansas City dollars. Them big cities, more folk, more demand - that's where the real money be at. But this here owner lady, she's good people. Fair wit' her prices, keeps her mouth shut tighter'n a tomb in winter."

Jesse nodded slowly. "Makes sense enough. Reckon I'm in for tomorrow night's delivery."

* * *

The summer sun beat down mercilessly as Tom dug at the stubborn stump blocking the irrigation ditch. Sweat soaked through his shirt, turning the fabric a darker shade as he worked the shovel around the thick root system. The physical labor felt good, keeping his mind focused on the present rather than drifting back to memories of France or the gnawing need for a drink.

Mary approached carrying a tin cup filled with fresh well water, her boots crunching on the dry earth. "Figured ya might could use somethin' cold to drink."

Tom straightened, wiping his forearm across his brow before accepting the cup gratefully. "Much obliged." He drank deeply, the cool water a blessing against the heat.

"Ya been doin' some right fine work these past few days," Mary said, watching him with approval. "Daddy would've sure 'preciated how thorough ya are with the irrigation."

"Thank ya kindly." Tom handed the cup back, then grabbed his shovel again. "Ever' farm needs good water flow."

"Been meanin' to ask - how ya been sleepin'? Any more of them nightmares?"

Tom paused, studying the troublesome stump. "Just the once, but that tea of yours helps settle things down right proper. Better'n the whiskey ever did."

"I'll fix ya up another batch to keep close by." Mary smiled, pleased he'd found some relief. She watched him struggle with the stump for a moment. "Shame that ol' stump's givin' ya such trouble."

"Don't s'pose ya got anythin' on the farm that might help pull this stubborn thing?" Tom asked, driving the shovel in for another attempt.

"Well, we got us a tractor, but it ain't run in months now." Mary sighed. "Just sittin' there collectin' dust."

Tom's eyes lit up. "Mind if I take me a look at 'er? Used to work on engines toward the end of the war."

The massive barn doors creaked open as Mary led Tom inside, sunlight streaming through gaps in the weathered wood. She moved purposefully toward a shape covered by a faded canvas tarp in the back corner. With a firm tug, she pulled the covering away, revealing the hulking form of a Rumely OilPull tractor.

"Well I'll be..." Tom breathed, running his hand along the rusted metal frame. The machine was impressive even in its current state of disrepair.

"Daddy bought 'er secondhand 'bout five years back," Mary explained, patting the huge back wheel."Come with enough kerosene to run 'er a good spell too. But after he passed..." She trailed off, her expression darkening. "Just sits here now, broke down an' useless."

Tom circled the tractor slowly, examining it from different angles. "Ya know much 'bout these contraptions?" Mary asked, watching him with interest.

"More'n I ever expected to," Tom replied. "Got myself banged up right bad in France - nothin' too serious, mind ya, but enough they transferred me to mechanical corps for a spell. Learned to fix 'bout anything with an engine." He crouched down to peer at the undercarriage. "Trucks, tanks, tractors - after a while they all start speakin' the same language."

"Ya really reckon ya could get 'er runnin' again?" Mary's voice held a note of cautious hope.

Tom straightened up, wiping his hands on his pants. "Won't know 'til I dig in and take me a proper look, but I reckon I can try. Might take a fair spell though."

"Time's all we got," Mary said. "Parts and money we ain't got a lick of."

Sarah entered the barn, a cloth-covered plate in her hands. "Brung y'all some Johnny Cakes for lunch," she called out, the sweet corn aroma filling the musty air.

Her eyes fell on the uncovered tractor. "What's all this about?"

"Tom here's gonna take a look, see if he can't fix 'er up," Mary explained, unable to hide her excitement. "He worked on engines durin' the war."

"Oh, that'd be wonderful!" Sarah's face lit up. "Been settin' here gatherin' dust far too long." She crossed the barn, holding out the plate to Tom. "Here ya go, fresh off the griddle."

"Much obliged, Mrs. Walker." Tom accepted two of the golden cakes with a grateful nod. He took a hearty bite, savoring the warm cornmeal.

Sarah walked back to stand beside Mary, but noticed her daughter's attention was fixed elsewhere. Following her gaze, she saw Tom setting his plate aside and pulling his sweat-soaked shirt over his head, revealing a lean, muscled torso marked by an angry scar across his back. He tossed the shirt aside and bent to open one of the tractor's side panels, muscles flexing as he worked the rusty bolts loose.

Sarah glanced at Mary, whose eyes remained glued to Tom's form. She gave her daughter a gentle elbow. "Don't look so hungry, ya heathen," she whispered with a knowing smile.

Mary's cheeks flushed crimson as she quickly looked away, but her eyes kept stealing glances back toward Tom as he began his inspection of the engine.

*　*　*

The afternoon sun had shifted as Tom lay beneath the massive OilPull, his hands working methodically at the stubborn bolts. The smell of grease and oil permeated the air after hours of work.

Mary's boots crunched on the dirt floor as she entered. "How's she comin' along?"

Tom slid out from under the tractor, his face and body streaked with black grease. He wiped his hands on an already filthy rag. Mary found herself stealing glances at his strong frame, her cheeks flushing red when he caught her looking as he turned to ask, "'Bout to find out if all this work paid off. Time to see if she'll turn over for us?"

"Oh! Um, yes," Mary managed, flustered by being caught staring.

He grabbed the side of the tractor with practiced ease, muscles tensing as he pulled himself up. Positioning his foot in the huge flywheel, he took a deep breath. "Here goes nothin'."

The first push met resistance, but Tom kept at it. Each forceful thrust of his leg sent the flywheel spinning further. A metallic clanking echoed through the barn as the engine slowly came to life. With one final powerful shove, the flywheel caught its rhythm, spinning freely as smoke began curling from the engine.

Mary clasped her hands together, bouncing on her toes as she let out an excited laugh. "Ya did it, Tom! Ya actually did it!"

Tom grinned down at her, pride evident on his oil-smeared face. "What say we go take care of that troublesome stump now?"

Tom wrapped the heavy chain around the base of the stump, his movements efficient and precise. The links clinked against each other as he secured the other end to the tractor's drawbar. Climbing into the seat, he adjusted the throttle and reached for the clutch.

The OilPull's engine roared to life, black smoke puffing from its exhaust. Tom eased forward until the chain pulled taut, then straightened the wheel. The tractor's massive wheels dug into the earth as he gave it more power.

For a moment, nothing happened. Then with a grinding crack, the stump's roots began to tear free. The tractor's engine bellowed as Tom opened the throttle wider. With a final heave, the stump ripped completely from the ground, sending clods of dirt flying.

Mary whooped and clapped as Tom killed the engine and hopped down to inspect their handiwork. The massive stump lay on its side, roots reaching skyward like gnarled fingers.

"That stump didn't stand a chance 'gainst this old girl." Tom said, patting the tractor's fender.

Mary shook her head, a smile playing at her lips. "Naw, that stump was no match for Tom Miller."

⁂

In the dimly lit chamber, Jesse watched as Bill filled the last jug of moonshine. The pungent smell of corn mash hung heavy in the air, mixing with the natural dampness of the cave.

"Ya bring that wagon like I done asked ya?" Bill wiped his hands on his overalls.

"It's hitched outside," Jesse nodded. "What's our strategy?"

Bill's eyes lit up as he explained, gesturing with weathered hands. "We'll load these jugs careful-like into the wagon, then take 'em down to the northeast corner of yer property, right where it meets the river. Got me a boat stashed there under some brush."

Jesse leaned against the cave wall, arms crossed. "And then?"

"We row upstream past the Riverside Inn," Bill continued, "Just past where that old mill burned down couple'a years back-"

Jesse's hand shot up, cutting Bill off mid-sentence. His body tensed, ears straining at a subtle sound echoing from the passageway - the slight scrape of boots on stone. In one fluid motion, he pulled his revolver from its holster and pointed it down the passageway.

Shadows danced on the cave walls as Jesse moved closer to the passage entrance, his voice carrying clear and strong through the chamber. "Whoever's lurkin', we know you're there. Show yourself, nice and easy."

The silence that followed seemed to stretch for an eternity, broken only by the steady drip of water somewhere in the darkness.

Tom emerged from the shadows, hands raised above his head. "Don't shoot, Jesse. It's just me."

Jesse lowered his gun but kept his stance rigid. "Tom? You been trackin' me?"

"I'm sorry," Tom shifted his weight. "Saw ya take the wagon from the barn, headin' this way. Mary mentioned you'd been comin' out here lately. Got the better of my curiosity, I s'pose."

Jesse slid the gun back into the holster, jaw clenched. "Now that you've stumbled onto our little enterprise, what's your mind set on?"

"I wanna help." Tom lowered his hands slowly. "Look, I know what it's like to lose everythin'. My family's farm got foreclosed while I was overseas. Couldn't do nothin' to stop it." He gestured at the stills. "If this is what it takes to save your place, I'm in. Consider it my way of showin' gratitude for everythin' you've done for me."

Bill cackled from his perch near the still. "Well butter my backside and call me a biscuit! 'Nother set of hands means my old bones can rest more. Been thinkin' 'bout retirin' from deliveries anyhow - arthritis makes rowin' that boat feel like wrestlin' a bear in church."

Jesse studied Tom's face, searching for any sign of deception. He found only determination and something familiar - that same haunted look they'd both brought back from France.

"You certain about this path?" Jesse asked. "Ain't exactly the kind of work that sits right with the law."

"Neither was half of what we done in the war," Tom replied. "Sometimes right and legal ain't the same thing."

Jesse stepped closer, his voice dropping low. "There's something else you need to understand. Mary and Mama - they can't know about any of this. I won't have them mixed up in it."

Tom nodded solemnly. "Course not. They got enough weighin' on them with the farm." He paused, understanding crossing his features. "I'll keep Mary's mind on other things - Lord knows there's plenty of work to be done in the daylight hours."

"Good," Jesse said. "Mary's been askin' questions about where I go. She's got sharp eyes and a sharper mind."

"Don't ya worry none about that," Tom assured him. "Between the crops needin' tendin' and the fences needin' mendin', I'll make sure she's got plenty to occupy her thoughts."

Jesse considered Tom for a long moment. He'd learned to read men during the war - to spot the liars, the cowards, the ones who'd break under pressure. Tom's expression held none of those tells. Still, trust was something earned slowly these days.

"Tell you what," Jesse said finally. "Help us with tonight's delivery. See what you're getting yourself into. After that, if you're still willing, we can talk about regular arrangements."

Bill nodded approvingly from his perch by the still. "Smart thinkin', boy. Let's see how steady his hands are 'fore we trust 'em with the good stuff."

Tom moved closer, boots crunching on the cave floor. The lantern light caught his face as he examined the stills with an expert eye. "Fair enough. My uncle ran a still back 'fore the law came down - this here's professional grade."

"Professional as a preacher on Sunday," Bill beamed with pride. "Now gather 'round boys, let ol' Bill tell ya how we're gonna make this delivery smooth as Tennessee whiskey."

The three men huddled near the warm copper still, their shadows merging into one dark shape against the cave wall as they began to plot their nocturnal venture. Jesse knew there'd be more conversations needed, more trust to be built, but for now, this would do.

* * *

Moonlight painted silver ribbons across the Finley River's surface as Tom carefully nestled the last ceramic jug between feed sacks in the johnboat. The craft was perfect for their needs - a flat-bottomed wooden vessel about sixteen feet long, narrow enough to slip through the shallows but stable enough to handle their cargo. Old quilts lined the bottom, muffling any tell-tale clinks of glass against wood.

"She's loaded and ready," Tom whispered, stepping back from the boat. "Everythin's secured."

Jesse nodded. "Take the wagon back to the barn. See that mare gets a proper rubdown - she's earned it."

Tom disappeared into the darkness with the wagon, the soft clip-clop of hooves fading into the night. Jesse and Bill pushed the johnboat into the current, the oars making barely a ripple as they began their journey upstream.

Whip-poor-wills called from the shoreline while bullfrogs added their deep chorus to the night music. The moon cast enough light to navigate, but shadows from the towering sycamores provided good cover along the banks.

"Tell me somethin', Bill," Jesse whispered between strokes of the oar, "How'd you come to be in this particular line of work?"

Bill chuckled softly, his voice carrying that peculiar Ozark lilt. "Wal, young feller, mah pappy was a whiskey man, 'n his'n afore him. Started me out when I weren't no bigger'n a minner in a wash bucket. Back then, hit was legal as scratchin' a tick bite."

"Reckon that stretches back a fair piece then?"

"Lawd yes! Lemme tell ye 'bout the time durin' the war - t'other war, mind ye - when I's a-totin' a batch to them Yankees what was camped down Wilson's Creek way. Their head feller, he traded me this here fancy timepiece fer three demijohns. Says it were pure gold." Bill paused to spit into the river. "Warn't nothin' but yeller brass, but I reckon the look on that Yankee's face when that shine hit his gullet were worth more'n any goldpiece ever minted."

Jesse couldn't help but smile. "You mean to tell me you were runnin' shine to Union boys?

"Young feller, durin' war, ever'body drinks the same whiskey."

* * *

The johnboat glided to a stop near the shoreline, just downstream from several other small craft moored in the shadows. Bill guided them to a secluded spot, away from the other boats. They dragged their vessel onto the muddy bank, careful not to let the jugs clank together.

"See that thar trail yonder?" Bill's gnarled finger pointed toward a thin path winding between the limestone bluffs. "Takes ye up to a holler in th' rock - that thar's th' Jumpin' Frog. Finest shine-house in these hyar parts, I tell ye true."

"What's next?" Jesse kept his voice low, scanning the darkness.

"I'll go jaw wit' 'em first-like. They'll send some young-uns down fer th' totin'." Bill tugged at his overalls. "You set right quiet-like, keep them eyes peeled sharp as a possum. Don't make nary a sound 'less'n ye hear our whistle."

Jesse melted into the underbrush near a giant oak as Bill's footsteps crunched up the path. The moon broke through the clouds, casting silver light across the riverside scene. Movement caught his eye - a figure emerging from the speakeasy trail.

The moonlight illuminated a familiar face. Jesse had to suppress a laugh as he recognized Luke, his straight-laced lawyer cousin, coming down from a backwoods liquor joint. *"Well, well,"* Jesse thought, *"Mr. High-and-Mighty ain't so proper after all."*

He watched as Luke turned right at the fork, taking a different path that wound uphill through the trees. Jesse nodded to himself - *must be where they park their motorcars, hidden from the main road.*

After a time, Bill's distinctive whistle pierced the night. Three shadowy figures followed him down the path.

"Jesse-boy, fetch them mason jars 'n foller after me," Bill called softly.

Jesse hefted several jugs and fell in behind them. The path wound upward between rocky walls until they reached what appeared to be a cabin built right into the cave mouth. A burly native man with forearms like tree trunks stood guard, a shotgun resting casually against his shoulder. He nodded at Bill and stepped aside.

The passage beyond was narrow but tall, their footsteps echoing off the damp stone. As they rounded a sharp bend, the cave opened into a chamber that took Jesse's breath away. Glass lanterns cast a warm glow across polished wooden tables where men gathered playing cards. Tobacco smoke curled toward the rocky ceiling. A weathered upright piano tinkled in the corner, its notes mixing with laughter and clinking glasses. Several women in short skirts and rouge-painted cheeks draped themselves across patrons' shoulders.

But it was the woman behind the ornate oak bar that caught Jesse's eye. High cheekbones and copper skin spoke of native blood, while her dark eyes held both intelligence and danger. Her black hair fell in waves past her shoulders, and she moved with the fluid grace of a mountain cat. Her clothing was a striking blend of styles - a finely tailored New Orleans dress modified with subtle Osage beadwork at the collar and cuffs. The combination somehow made perfect sense, like the woman herself.

"Rose!" Bill hollered. "This hyar's Jesse Walker, ol' James's boy whut I been tellin' ye 'bout!" He turned to Jesse with a grin. "Jesse, meet Miss Rose Thorne. She runs this hyar fine 'stablishment, an' don't let her purty face fool ya - she's sharp as a thorn an' twice as dangerous as a rattler in July."

"Pleasure to make your acquaintance," Jesse said, extending his hand.

"Enchantée, Monsieur Walker," Rose replied, as she studied him carefully. "Tell me, how does a soldier plan to move shine without gettin' caught?"

"Same principles as movin' supplies through German lines - know your ground, study your enemy's habits, always keep a fallback route in your pocket." Jesse paused. "Though I suspect you already know the best paths 'round here, being Osage."

A smile played at her lips. "Not many catch that, cher. Bill's right about you - there might be hope yet." She poured three glasses of amber liquid. "Have a seat while my boys bring in your delivery. This one's on la maison."

Rose disappeared behind the extended bar wall into what appeared to be an office. Jesse settled onto a bar stool next to Bill, taking in the lively atmosphere of the cave speakeasy.

When Rose returned, she handed Jesse a thick envelope. "Payment for the shipment."

"Much obliged," Jesse said, tucking it into his jacket.

Rose turned to Bill. "Next month, I'm needin' double the usual amount."

"Twice?" Bill scratched at his whiskers like a hound with fleas. "Reckon we kin do it, but what in tarnation's got into ye, girl?"

"Lost one of my suppliers last week. Whole operation wiped out."

Jesse straightened. "These shine-runners you lost - did they have a still out James River way?"

Rose's eyes narrowed. "How'd you know about that?"

"Come across the aftermath, like finding a battlefield after the shooting's done," Jesse said. "Heard the gunfire echoin' off the bridge on my way back from Springfield. Found some fellows loadin' equipment and shine into one of them new Ford trucks. One poor devil was still breathin' - managed to tell me it was the Finley River boys before he passed."

Rose slammed her fist on the bar. "Merde! Bastards pickin' off every small operation they can find, like wolves cullin' the weak."

"Cuts into your trade?" Jesse asked.

"Without competition, prices soar higher than an eagle," Rose's jaw tightened. "And those Finley River cochons - they won't sell to anyone whose blood ain't pure as their precious white lightnin'."

"Any other operations still runnin' these hills?" Jesse asked.

"About a dozen small operations left." Rose lowered her voice. "Finley River Gang's the biggest, but there's another force movin' through these hills. Don't know much, 'cept the Finley boys won't touch them. Must have serious muscle and deep pockets, and they don't sell local." She fixed them both with a hard stare. "Watch yourselves. Finley Gang's always huntin' new territory."

Bill pushed back from the bar. "Them playin' cards is singin' sweeter'n a camp meetin' choir."

"Keep your britches buttoned this time, mon ami," Rose called after him. "Last week's show scared half my clientèle."

Jesse chuckled as Bill wandered off, already humming another nonsensical tune.

"I'm sorry 'bout your father," Rose said, her voice softening. James was good people."

"Much obliged. Seems everybody knew him better'n I did these past few years." Jesse shifted the conversation. "What brought you to the Ozark hills?"

Rose pulled out two fresh glasses, filling them with amber liquid. "Life flows like the river, cher - you never know where it'll take you. Born in New Orleans myself - my mama left these hills for the city, fell in love with my papa who ran one of the finest jazz clubs on Basin Street." Her voice carried that distinctive Louisiana lilt tinged with something older, more native to these hills. "Lost them both to the fever before I was married. Then when my husband died in the war, I came back here to care for my grandmother. She was the one who taught my mama the old Osage ways, still lived on the family land." She traced the rim of her glass. "When she passed, wasn't much work to be found - especially for someone with skin like mine. But I had my husband's insurance money and grandmother's wisdom about these hills. Found some like-minded folks who didn't care what color you were, long as you had sense and strength."

"Opening an illegal business," Jesse mused. "Either mighty brave or mighty crazy. Having met you, I'm betting on the former."

A smile played at her lips. "And you, cher? What's your opinion on operating outside the law?"

"During the war, we learned quick that survival and legality don't always walk the same path," Jesse said. "Sometimes the right thing ain't necessarily the legal thing."

Rose studied him thoughtfully. "Your daddy mentioned you stayed in Europe after the war. What kept you there?"

"Needed time to sort myself out after France. Wandered some, buried myself in books. Even worked a spell at a vineyard near Bordeaux - though their wine ain't got the same kick as your whiskey here."

Rose's dark eyes studied him with interest. "A soldier who knows fine wine? Mon dieu, you're just full of surprises, aren't you, cher?"

"Speakin' of surprises - you favor Mark Twain's stories?"

Her eyebrows lifted, her New Orleans drawl becoming more pronounced. "Mais oui, that clever little name above my door give it away?"

"The Celebrated Jumping Frog of Calaveras County," Jesse smiled. "Not many would catch that particular reference in these hills. Story's about a man who'd bet on anything - even trained his frog to jump higher than any other. Until someone filled that poor frog's belly with quail shot when he wasn't looking."

"Seems fittin' for a speakeasy, non?" Rose said, a gleam in her eye. "Some folks might try to weigh me down with their tricks, just like that frog. But this chere has learned to check for shot in her pockets. I'll outjump anyone fool enough to bet against me, I guarantee."

Their eyes held for a moment longer than necessary, both understanding the deeper meaning behind her words. In these dangerous times, survival meant staying one step ahead of those who'd try to drag you down. Rose finally turned to serve another customer, the musical lilt of her "Merci, cher" floating back to Jesse as she walked away.

6

Buffalo and Bull

Jesse sat on a wooden crate in the cave chamber, watching Bill check the latest batch of moonshine with an expert's eye. The pungent smell of corn mash filled the air as Tom leaned against the cave wall, his military posture evident even in repose. The orange glow from the fire beneath the stills cast dancing shadows on the limestone walls, making the cave seem alive with movement. Steam hissed occasionally from the copper coils, adding to the cave's ethereal atmosphere.

"Got us a week ta figger how we's gonna haul this hyar hundred-fifty gallons up Bolivar way," Bill said, holding a jar up to the firelight and swirling the clear shine inside. "That's whar my Kansas City boys does their buyin', sure as a possum loves persimmons."

Jesse pulled his pipe from his pocket, stuffing it with tobacco from the small tin he'd carried since France. "That's a fair piece to transport, no doubt about it. Wagon ain't gonna serve - them jars'd be more broke than whole by journey's end. To quote old Julius Caesar: 'Swift as the wind, else our venture fails.' Six days there and back's more time than we can spare."

"I saw an Atterbury truck fer sale in town." Tom said, straightening up with renewed interest. "Down at Halloway's Mercantile. Might be worth checkin' out. It's one of them models with the enclosed cab."

Jesse struck a match, puffing his pipe to life as he considered Tom's suggestion. The sweet Virginia blend mixed with shine vapors, bringing back memories of being in French dugouts. "Might be you've hit on somethin' there, Tom." He paused, studying his friend. "Mary ain't caught wind of any of this, has she?"

Tom shook his head. "She's asked why you come out here so much. Told her sometimes after war, a man needs space to heal. She understood right quick - said she wouldn't pry."

"Good," Jesse nodded. "Ma's easier - keeps herself busy with the house and garden. Barely notices I'm gone most days."

"Reckon we best be thinkin' 'bout that truck," Bill drawled, settin' the jar back among the others. "Them Atterburys is good strong wagons - won't catch nary an eye, seein' as how ever' farmer 'round these hyar parts got one. Been spottin' 'em all over these hills, sure as the Lord made little green apples."

"Could make the run in half a day tops," Tom added, his mechanical expertise showing through. "Specially if we tune up the engine proper."

Jesse exhaled a cloud of smoke, watching it drift up toward the cave ceiling where it mingled with the steam from the stills. "Reckon we'd best go see about that truck then." His mind was already working through the logistics of the purchase and how to explain it to his mother and sister.

* * *

Jesse and Tom rode their horses down Church Street in Ozark, the clip-clop of hooves echoing off the storefronts. Jesse looked up at the gathering clouds, dark and heavy with promise.

"Weather's fixin' to turn," he said, adjusting his flat cap against the rising wind.

Tom nodded, studying the sky. "Yep, storm's brewin' fer sure. Can smell it in the air. Sure hope it comes our way - corn's needin' water somethin' fierce."

"Jesse Walker! Lord above, ain't you a sight!" Mrs. Adams called from the dress shop doorway, her silver hair catching the wind. "You tell that mama of yours to come by for Sunday dinner soon!"

Jesse tipped his cap with a smile. A few doors down, old Doc Wilson looked up from sweeping his porch, offering a knowing nod. "Welcome home, son. I must say, it does my old heart good to see you returned to us safe and sound."

They reached Halloway's Mercantile and hitched their horses to the post out front as a couple of Model Ts puttered past, their engines chugging in that familiar rhythm. Young Billy Cooper ran past with his friends, stopping short when he recognized Jesse. "Mr. Walker! You gonna teach us to shoot straight like you promised 'fore the war?"

Jesse chuckled, "Reckon when you're a mite older, Billy boy."

The bell above the door chimed as they entered the store, the wooden floorboards creaking beneath their boots. Jesse felt a warmth in his chest – the Ozarks might've changed some, but its people were still the same good folk he remembered. Simple, honest people who looked after their own.

"Well, if it ain't Tom Miller," Mr. Halloway called from behind the counter, his round spectacles catching the light. "Right pleased to see ya standin' steady fer once."

"Mr. Halloway," Tom replied with a respectful nod.

Jesse stepped forward, extending his hand. "Mr. Halloway, pleasure to cross paths again."

"Jesse Walker," the shopkeeper's face softened. "Shore was grieved to hear 'bout your daddy. James, he always dealt square with folks 'round here."

"Much obliged, sir," Jesse said, shaking the offered hand. "Truth is, word's reached me about an Atterbury you're lookin' to part with. Thought we might have a look, if you're amenable."

"That I do," Mr. Halloway brightened, wiping his hands on his apron. "C'mon 'round back, I'll show ya what I got." He fetched his key ring from under the counter. "Fella couldn't pay his store bill, traded it to me last year."

They followed the shopkeeper through the store, past shelves stocked with dry goods and farming supplies, and out the back door into the yard.

Behind the store sat an Atterbury 7D, its battleship gray paint dulled by months of sun and rain. Despite its worn appearance, Jesse could see the truck's potential beneath the grime.

"What brings you to sell such a fine piece of machinery?" Jesse asked, running his hand along the hood.

"Ain't run fer over six months," Halloway sighed. "Can't see payin' them fancy Springfield mechanics what they's askin' to look at it. Rather get shut of it and call it done."

"Mind if Tom takes a gander? He's got quite the gift with engines - learned it in the motor pool over in France."

"Be my guest," Halloway waved at the truck. As Tom lifted the hood, the shopkeeper glanced around and lowered his voice. "Say, Jesse, while we're standin' here - ya heard any talk 'bout Sheriff Hayes lately? Seen him comin' outta Richmond's bank yesterday. Third time this week. Mighty peculiar, seein' as how Hayes fought so hard against Richmond buyin' up the old bank last year."

"Can't rightly speak to local matters," Jesse said, watching Tom work. "Only been back home these past couple weeks." He paused thoughtfully. "Though I appreciate you keepin' me informed, Mr. Halloway. Town's changed some since I left."

Jesse kept his expression placid, though his mind quickened at the news. Tom's gesture drew him to the engine.

"What's your assessment?" Jesse asked.

"Simple fix," Tom said quietly. "Magneto's out of adjustment. Most folks wouldn't catch it, but I've seen it 'fore. Hour's work, tops."

Jesse turned back to Halloway. "What figure you got in mind?"

"Thousand dollars, and that's firm as oak."

Jesse barked out a laugh. "A thousand? For an automobile that won't run? Beggin' your pardon, Mr. Halloway, but that's highway robbery."

"Now see here-"

"Well now," Jesse stepped back, stance casual but calculated, "reckon we'll have to decline. Shame too - was hopin' to strike a bargain."

"Hold on, hold on," Halloway raised his hands. "Might be I spoke too quick. How'd four hundred strike ya?"

"Now that," Jesse smiled, "sounds like terms worth explorin'."

* * *

"I'll have 'er purrin' by sundown," Tom said, patting the truck's hood. "You take the horses back."

Jesse nodded, trusting Tom's mechanical aptitude. He stepped back into Halloway's store, the wooden floor creaking under his boots. At the counter, he counted out four hundred dollars, watching Mr. Halloway's eyes widen at the stack of bills.

"And some of them Cherry Chasers," Jesse added, pointing to the glass jar of candies.

Mr. Halloway scooped out a handful, wrapping them in paper. Jesse popped one in his mouth, savoring the sweet cherry flavor as he walked to the window. The courthouse stood across the street, its brick facade catching the afternoon light.

Sheriff Hayes appeared on the courthouse steps, his uniform pressed and badge catching the sun. Mr. Wilcox from the Richmond bank approached him, his shoulders hunched and eyes darting. Jesse watched as the loan officer's trembling hands reached into his pocket, producing a folded piece of paper. Hayes took it without a word, stuffing it into his uniform as Wilcox scurried away like a spooked rabbit.

The sheriff adjusted his gun belt and strode off in the opposite direction, leaving Jesse to wonder what kind of business a loan officer and sheriff could have that required such an exchange.

Jesse stepped out of Halloway's, spotting Hayes' uniform moving down the street. He kept his distance, staying behind wagons and groups of townspeople as he followed. The sheriff's purposeful stride suggested he had somewhere specific to be.

A woman's scream pierced the air from behind the row of shops. "Stop! Don't hurt him!"

Jesse hesitated, glancing between Hayes' retreating figure and the direction of the commotion. The woman's voice rang out again, desperate and afraid. He cursed under his breath and ducked into the narrow alley between Morton's Feed Store and the cobbler's shop.

Behind the buildings, four men in dirty overalls had cornered their prey. One thug gripped a young black woman by her arms as she struggled. The other three surrounded a black man about Jesse's age, taking turns landing blows.

"Where's that Rose-gal git her shine at?" The ringleader spat, driving his fist into the man's ribs. "We knows you works fer that Injun woman. Tell us who's providin' them shipments."

The black man stayed silent, blood trickling from his split lip.

"Better start flappin' them lips," the ringleader sneered, "or yer jigaboo here's gonna find out what real mountain boys does to folks like her."

Rage flashed across the black man's face. He lunged forward, catching the leader with a solid right hook. He dodged another attacker's swing and landed a punch to his gut. But the third man tackled him from behind, and soon all three had him pinned to the dirt.

Jesse stepped forward from the shadows. "Might want to reconsider your position while you still have the choice."

The leader spun around, spitting tobacco juice. "Well, ain't you the hero? There's four of us and one of you. What's your stake in this? You sweet on darkies?"

"I'd take their fellowship over yours any day given," Jesse's eyes locked onto the dog tags glinting around the black man's neck. "What's your name, soldier?"

"Virgil Coffey, suh," the man answered through bloodied lips.

"Served in the Great War, did you, Virgil?"

"Yessuh, I did. Sho' did."

"Which outfit?"

"92nd Infantry Division, suh."

Jesse's eyebrows raised. "I'll be damned."

"Hey! We ain't done here-" the leader started.

"This here's one of them Buffalo Soldiers, you addled fool," Jesse cut him off. "His regiment cut through the Western Front like summer lightning. Heard tell of their valor at Meuse-Argonne. Rough business, wasn't it, Virgil?"

"Dat it was, suh. Lost a heap of good men over dere."

Jesse turned back to the leader. "Course, you wouldn't know nothin' about that. Don't appear to be acquainted with the written word."

The leader's face twisted in rage as he swung a wild haymaker. Jesse slipped the punch and dropped him with a quick right cross. The second man charged, catching a knee to the gut that doubled him over. Jesse grabbed his collar and slung him into the third attacker. The fourth man released the woman and pulled a knife, but Jesse was already moving. He trapped the knife hand and snapped the man's wrist with a sharp twist. The blade clattered to the ground as the thug howled in pain.

The remaining men scrambled to their feet and fled, dragging their unconscious leader with them.

Jesse helped Virgil to his feet as the woman rushed forward, her hands fluttering over Virgil's bruised face.

"It's awright, Edith. I'ma be fine," Virgil assured her, wiping blood from his lip.

"Much obliged fo' steppin' in when you did," Virgil said, turning to Jesse. "Mighta ended pow'ful different otherwise."

"Who were those men?" Jesse brushed dirt from his sleeves.

"Finley River Gang." Virgil spat blood. "Reckon dey thought dey could beat Miz Rose's supplier list outta me."

"The Jumping Frog? Then you're one of Rose's people?"

"So you've been there?" Virgil's eyebrows lifted.

Jesse nodded but offered nothing more.

"Dem boys is desperate to wipe out de competition." Virgil wrapped an arm around Edith's shoulders. "Been hittin' every operation dey can find, tryin' to control everythin' dat flows through these hills."

"Rose mentioned something of the sort." Jesse pulled out his handkerchief and handed it to Virgil. "Listen here - ever find yourself needin' safe harbor, our farm's just outside town a few miles. Walker place - can't miss it."

"Dat's mighty kind of you, suh." Virgil dabbed at his split lip. "Might hafta take you up on dat someday."

* * *

Jesse walked through the wrought iron gates of the Ozark Cemetery, his boots crunching on the gravel path. The afternoon sun beat down on the open hillside, where rows of weathered headstones stretched toward the horizon. The July heat shimmered off the markers, but a gentle breeze carried the sweet scent of summer grass.

He passed familiar names carved in stone - Henrys, Gundersons, Hansons- families that had called these hills home for generations.

Some dates went back to before the Civil War, telling silent stories of lives lived and lost in these highlands.

Then he saw it - a stone still crisp and white against the weathered gray markers surrounding it. Young grass had begun to take root over the grave, nature's way of healing the torn earth. Jesse's throat tightened as he read the inscription:

JAMES WALKER 1867 - 1923 Beloved Husband & Father "The righteous man walks in his integrity" Proverbs 20:7

He stood there for a long moment, hands in his pockets, searching for words that wouldn't come. The war had taught him to face death unflinching, but this was different. This was home, this was family.

Finally, he cleared his throat. "Sorry it took me so long to visit, Daddy." The word came naturally, as it always had between them. To everyone else, he'd been 'Father' - Jesse had made sure of that since he was old enough to understand what respect meant, wanting the world to know the measure of the man who'd raised him. His voice came out rough. "Got your letter from Bill. You were right about him - he's quite a character."

Jesse shifted his weight, adjusting his flat cap - a nervous habit he'd picked up from his father. "Never thought I'd see the day when James Walker turned moonshiner. But these past weeks, trying to save the farm…" He shook his head. "Well, I understand why. You did what you had to for family. Reckon I'm following those footsteps, though maybe not the way you'd have wanted."

He knelt down, fingers tracing the carved letters of his father's name. "That last thing I said before leaving - about you being a bitter old man wasting away growing corn. I was wrong. Young fool's words, thinking I knew better than generations of Walker wisdom. You had your ways, and I respect them now. Learned the hard way that a man's honor means more than all the gold in creation."

Jesse stood, dusting off his knees. "Mary's strong as ever - just like you always said she'd be. And Mama… well, she misses you something fierce, but she's got that same Walker steel in her spine." He paused, fighting back the thickness in his throat. "We're holding together, Daddy. Keeping the family name strong, just like you taught us."

For a long moment, he stood silent before the headstone. The summer sky stretched endless above him, that deep Ozark blue that his daddy had loved so much. Jesse's gaze dropped back to the grave, remembering how many times he'd seen his father standing in their cornfields, face turned up to that same sky with quiet pride in the land he worked.

As he finally turned to leave, a strong breeze swept across the hillside, warm and gentle as a father's touch, and something tight in his chest loosened. Maybe it was imagination, but in that moment, Jesse felt his father's forgiveness as surely as if he'd heard that deep, familiar laugh carried on the summer wind.

"I'll make it right, Daddy," he whispered. "I promise you that."

* * *

The sunset painted the Ozark hills in brilliant orange and gold, casting long shadows across the Walker Farm. Those promising storm clouds from earlier had drifted north, leaving Ozark and its surroundings still hot and dry despite Tom's hopes. Jesse latched the heavy wooden barn door, satisfied after getting the horses settled in their stalls for the night. The earthy smell of hay and leather filled his nostrils as he patted the worn planks of the barn, weathered by decades of summer storms and winter frost.

The crunch of tires on gravel caught his attention. A familiar put-put sound grew louder as Tom guided the Atterbury truck down the dirt driveway, the engine purring smoothly. He brought it to a stop near the barn, a proud grin spread across his oil-smudged face.

"Well now, ain't that something," Jesse said, walking over to inspect the truck. "Reckon you've proved your worth twice over, Tom. Got a real gift when it comes to fixin' machines."

Tom hopped down from the driver's seat, wiping his hands on a rag. "Like I said, simple fix once ya know what yer lookin' fer. Jest needed some time to git it right." He ran his hand along the truck's hood with obvious satisfaction.

"Better get washed up," Jesse said, catching the scent of his mother's cooking drifting from the farmhouse. "Mama's got supper near ready."

Jesse walked into the house, the wooden floorboards creaking beneath his boots. Mary sat curled in their father's old leather chair, her face buried in the newspaper. The aroma of salt pork and fried potatoes wafted from the kitchen where their mother worked on supper.

Mary lowered the paper. "Where'd ya git that truck?"

"Found it at Halloway's store in town at a fair price. Tom worked his magic and got it goin'"

"How'd ya pay fer it?" Mary folded the newspaper in her lap.

Jesse hung his hat on the rack. "Put some of that saved army pay to good use. Figured it'll serve double duty - haulin' corn come harvest and..." he paused, choosing his words like picking ripe fruit, "other enterprises that might help keep the farm."

"We ain't gonna have the farm come harvest time." The bitterness in Mary's voice cut through the air.

"Then I reckon it'll haul our belongings elsewhere," Jesse snapped. He rubbed his face, instantly regretting the words. "That was poorly said - my temper got the better of my tongue, apologies."

"No, I'm sorry too." Mary smoothed her skirt. "Ya figured out anythin' yet? 'Bout payin' off that debt?"

"Working on it." Jesse loosened his collar.

"Luke come by earlier whilst you was out." Mary pointed toward their father's roll-top desk. "Left ya a note over there."

Jesse walked to his father's roll-top desk, the aged wood smooth beneath his fingers as he lifted the curved top. Luke's note lay prominently on top of scattered papers. He unfolded it, recognizing his cousin's precise handwriting:

"Jesse - Need your help. I have a court case wrapping up in two days that could turn ugly. Would appreciate having you there to watch my back. Will pay well for your time. I'll stop by tomorrow to discuss details. - Luke"

As Jesse set the note down, another letter caught his eye - his father's distinctive scrawl jumped out from beneath some old receipts. His heart quickened as he pulled it free. The paper was dated just one day before his father's death:

"Meeting Hayes at Finley Cave tonight. Time to settle things once and for all. If anything happens to me..."

The words trailed off, as if his father had been interrupted mid-thought. Jesse's hands tightened on the paper, creasing its edges. The sheriff's story about an anonymous tip suddenly felt hollow. His father had planned to meet Hayes there - the same place where his body was found.

Jesse folded the letter carefully and slipped it into his shirt pocket, his mind racing with implications. The timing was too perfect to be coincidence. The late evening heat pressed down on the farmhouse, the air still and heavy from another rainless day.

"Sure is a scorcher," Mary said, fanning herself with an old newspaper. "Tom better come in soon 'fore he melts out there."

Jesse barely heard her, his thoughts fixed on Hayes and his father. The sheriff's convenient discovery of the body, the anonymous tip that led him straight there - it all felt wrong. And now this note proved his father had arranged to meet Hayes that night.

The front door opened as Tom walked in, wiping sweat from his brow with his sleeve. "Ain't no breeze out there at all." He dropped heavily into a chair.

"They's water in the kitchen," Sarah called. "Fresh from the well."

Beyond the windows, heat shimmered above the dusty yard, and the cicadas buzzed their endless summer song, a constant reminder of the sun's grip on the farm.

Jesse touched the letter through his shirt pocket. Whatever happened between Hayes and his father that night, the truth was out there. But first, he had Luke's note to deal with. His cousin wasn't one to ask for help lightly - especially not the kind that might turn ugly.

7

A Matter of Justice

Jesse watched the streets of Springfield roll past, his elbow resting on the Model T's open window frame. The city had grown since he'd left - more automobiles crowded the streets, their exhaust mixing with the sweet scent of fresh-baked bread from Meyer's Bakery. A trolley clanged its bell as it passed, the wheels screeching against iron rails.

Luke sat rigid behind the wheel, his pressed suit immaculate despite the summer heat. The gold watch chain across his vest caught the morning sun. Jesse felt distinctly underdressed in his work shirt and suspenders.

"Much obliged for the company," Luke said, navigating around a horse-drawn wagon. "Judge White moved the trial up here from Ozark - said Christian County had too many farmers, too much sympathy for Weber's situation. Can't say I blame him. Even here in Greene County, sentiment's running rather high." He adjusted his silk tie with manicured fingers. "I'd rest easier with you standing sentinel."

"Tell me more about this Weber fellow," Jesse said.

"John Weber - held a farmstead north of Finley River. Bank initiated foreclosure proceedings six months ago due to payment delinquency."

Luke's knuckles whitened on the steering wheel. "When Michael Collins, the agent of repossession, arrived to serve notice and take possession, Weber…" Luke's careful city accent slipped slightly. "Well, he shot him dead where he stood."

"Cold blood?" Jesse asked.

"Didn't speak a word, just pulled the trigger." Luke shook his head. "Collins left a wife, three young children. Simply executing his lawful duty."

The courthouse loomed before them, its classical revival façade stretching skyward. Jesse stepped out of the Model T, taking in the crowd that had gathered - farmers in dusty overalls, women in simple cotton dresses, storekeepers and laborers all mingling together. Their angry voices carried across the courthouse lawn.

"Weber ain't no killer!" someone shouted. "Bank drove him to it!"

"Justice for honest folks!" called another.

Luke adjusted his tie as they climbed the wide stone steps. "Stay close," he muttered. "These people are powder kegs waiting for a spark."

They passed through the arched doorway into the courthouse proper. Jesse's boots clicked against the marble floor as he glanced up at the ornate ceiling, with its detailed crown molding and painted trim. Morning light from the tall windows cast shifting patterns across the polished stone interior.

The main floor was chaos - clerks darting between desks with stacks of papers, lawyers huddled in corners with clients, bailiffs trying to maintain order as more protesters pushed their way inside. The marble stairs leading to the upper floors were packed with people moving up and down like ants on a hill.

"Make way! Coming through!" A harried-looking deputy muscled past, leading a handcuffed man toward the holding cells.

"Mr. Weber is being brought up presently," Luke said, checking his pocket watch. "We should head to the courtroom."

Jesse nodded, keeping his eyes on the crowd. He noticed several men with weathered faces and calloused hands watching Luke with barely concealed hostility. The tension in the air was thick enough to cut with a knife.

Luke shouldered past the reporters clustered outside the courtroom doors, their pencils scratching against notepads as they peppered him with questions. Jesse followed close behind, studying the ornate woodwork and high ceiling of the courtroom as they entered. Rows of wooden benches stretched from wall to wall, every seat filled with spectators pressed shoulder to shoulder.

The late July heat hung heavy in the air despite the tall windows being thrown wide open. Ladies fanned themselves with folded papers while men mopped their brows with handkerchiefs. A welcome breeze stirred the cotton curtains, bringing momentary relief to the stifling chamber.

Jesse's infantry training kicked in as he scanned the crowd, watching for sudden movements. The gallery was packed tight - farmers in sweat-stained shirts, merchants in rolled-up sleeves, women in their Sunday best despite the heat. The air crackled with tension and unspoken anger.

They made their way to the prosecution's table near the judge's bench. Jesse remained standing as Luke took his seat and arranged his papers. The carved wooden railings and polished brass fixtures spoke of authority and justice, but Jesse couldn't shake the feeling that today those ideals might not matter. Too many desperate faces filled the room, too many people who saw their own struggles reflected in John Weber's fate.

A clock on the wall ticked steadily toward ten, each movement bringing them closer to the moment when twelve men would decide Weber's fate. Jesse flexed his hands, forcing himself to stay relaxed but ready as the murmur of the crowd grew louder with anticipation.

* * *

Jesse sat behind Luke, close enough to keep an eye on him. Luke pulled out his watch and checked the time, his face was that of pure concentration, he wasn't shaky, he was confident. "All rise for the Honorable Judge John Turner White." Said the bailiff. The courtroom stood and waited as the judge took his seat and they sat at his command. The judge ordered the jury to take their places and Luke took the podium and called John Weber to the witness stand.

John Weber sat at the witness stand, a man in his late fifties, he wore his shabby farming clothes proudly. His wife sat in the front row, desperately trying to fight back the tears as family gathered around her. Jesse had seen that look in her eye, it was the same look Jesse's mother had at times, worrying if her family would keep the farm or be forced to vacate the only home they've known. Jesse felt sorry for them.

Weber took his oath, weathered hand raised as sunlight cut through the dusty courtroom air. His face held deep lines carved by years working the land, but his eyes burned with a defiance that made several jurors shift uncomfortably in their seats. The wooden witness chair creaked as he settled his lean frame into it.

Luke approached with measured steps, his polished shoes clicking against the floorboards. "Mr. Weber, kindly relate to the court the events of January twelfth," he said, voice carrying clear through the hushed room.

Weber's hands gripped the witness stand railing. "Was my land. Four gen'rations worked that there soil." His voice cracked slightly. "Feller shows up with them fancy papers, tellin' me I got one hour ta clear out. One hour ta pack up a lifetime."

"That individual was Michael Collins," Luke stated with calculated formality. "The deceased by your hand."

A murmur rippled through the crowd. Jesse noticed several men in the gallery nodding grimly, as if Weber's actions made perfect sense. The judge rapped his gavel once, restoring order.

Luke straightened his tie and began laying out the established facts. The timeline was precise, methodical - just like everything else about Luke's prosecution. Jesse shifted in his seat as his cousin's voice filled the stuffy courtroom.

"Bank documentation clearly indicates a complete absence of payment for six consecutive months prior to foreclosure proceedings," Luke declared, holding up a leather-bound ledger.

Weber's face reddened. "That ain't nowheres near true! I made them payments reg'lar as Sunday preachin'! Richmond Bank done lost 'em or throwed 'em away, sure as I'm standin' here!"

Jesse's spine stiffened at the mention of Richmond Bank. His fingers dug into his thighs as he realized this was the same bank threatening his family's land.

Luke produced a stack of letters with flourish. "These communications paint quite a different picture, Mr. Weber. Perhaps you'd care to elaborate on these written threats directed toward the banking institution?"

Weber's weathered face fell as Luke read from the stack of letters. "'You thievin' sons of devils won't get away with this. The Lord sees what yer doing to honest folk.'" Luke shuffled to another letter. "'Mr. Richmond, you keep pushin' folk too far, someday somebody's gonna push back. Mark my words.'" Jesse watched his cousin work, dismantling Weber's defense piece by piece with surgical precision. The skill was impressive - and terrifying.

"Sheriff Hayes was right there!" Weber burst out. "He seen me make least two of them payments they's claimin' never happened. An' that mornin', when that Collins feller showed up without no warnin'..." Weber's voice cracked. "Hayes, he tried to settle things down-like, told me ta take me a walk whilst he jaw'd with Collins."

"Pray continue," Luke pressed.

"Collins, he followed me out ta the barn. Tried ta take my pistol away from me. We scuffled 'round and…" Weber's shoulders slumped. "Gun went off. I swear on my mama's grave, I never meant fer none of it ta happen…"

"No additional questions, your honor," Luke said smoothly.

As Weber trudged back to his attorney, his voice rose. "Them banks is stealin' ever'thing from us folk!"

"The court calls Sheriff Marcus Hayes to the stand," Luke announced, cutting off Weber's outburst.

Sheriff Hayes took the stand, his uniform pressed and badge gleaming in the sunlight that streamed through the tall windows. He placed his hand on the Bible, swore his oath, then settled into the witness chair with practiced ease.

"Sheriff, please recount for the court the events of the morning in question," Luke began.

"I generally send my deputies along when the bank comes callin'," Hayes explained, his voice carrying authority. "This particular instance, though, I chose to ride with young Collins myself."

"And your observations upon arrival at the scene?"

"Mr. Weber, he looked like he'd been struck by lightning when they told him about them missing payments," Hayes said. "Kept saying over and over, 'Marcus, you know I wouldn't miss payments. There's been some manner of mistake here.'"

Luke paced before the witness stand. "Prior to said incident, were you made aware of any threats Mr. Weber had issued against the banking institution?"

"That's correct," Hayes nodded. "Had reports of both spoken and written threats against the institution."

"And you can verify, Sheriff, that you never personally witnessed Mr. Weber making these alleged payments?"

Hayes shifted slightly. "Saw him regular, many a time, heading into that bank on payment days. But can't rightly say I ever witnessed him making the actual deposits."

"Then it stands to reason," Luke pressed, "that Mr. Weber's claims of payment are entirely unsubstantiated?"

"Now that's something I couldn't rightfully swear to either way," Hayes said.

Weber exploded from his seat. "You know good an' well I made them payments, Marcus!"

The gavel cracked like a gunshot. "Mr. Weber, sit down immediately or I'll hold you in contempt!" Judge White thundered.

Weber's attorneys grabbed his arms, whispering urgently as they guided him back to his seat. "Let us handle this," they insisted, forcing him down.

Luke turned back to Hayes. "Sheriff, did you observe any evidence of Mr. Collins engaging in a struggle for the firearm in Mr. Weber's possession?"

"No sir, I did not." Hayes adjusted his collar. "Heard the gunshot, and by the time I made it to that barn…" He paused, his voice taking on an official tone. "Weber was standing there with the weapon, and Collins was deceased at the scene."

"No further questions for this witness, your honor," Luke said, returning to his seat.

Weber's attorney rose slowly, shoulders already slumped in defeat. "Sheriff Hayes, isn't it true that you've known Mr. Weber for over twenty years?"

"Objection, relevance," Luke called out.

"Sustained," Judge White ruled.

"Sheriff Hayes, did Mr. Weber ever show violent tendencies before this incident?"

"Objection, speculation."

"Sustained. Counselor, stick to the facts of the case."

Weber's attorney sat down, defeated. The judge called for closing arguments.

Weber's lawyer stood, his voice wavering. "Gentlemen, John Weber is a family man, a pillar of his community. Four generations of Webers worked that land. Would such a man throw it all away in cold blood?"

Luke rose next, commanding the jury's attention. "The evidence before this court is unambiguous, gentlemen. Six months of documented payment delinquency. A series of increasingly hostile communications. And when Mr. Collins arrived to execute his lawful duty…" He paused for effect. "Mr. Weber responded with lethal force. Sheriff Hayes discovered him still holding the murder weapon. These facts, gentlemen, stand incontrovertible."

Judge White turned to the jury. "You have heard the evidence. You will now retire to deliberate your verdict. Court is in recess."

The jury filed out as a fresh wave of tension filled the stuffy courtroom. Jesse watched them go, his mind racing with uncomfortable parallels to his own family's situation.

*   *   *

Jesse made his way over to Luke as the courtroom began its recess. "You're a different creature altogether up there on that podium," Jesse said. "Put me in mind of them Roman orators I read about - fierce as a mountain cat when you're at it."

Luke straightened his papers, tapping them into a neat stack. "Part of the profession, Jesse. Can't let personal considerations cloud legal obligations."

"How long you figure before the jury renders their verdict?"

"Could be hours," Luke replied, slipping his fountain pen into his breast pocket. "These country juries…" He caught himself, straightened his tie. "The local jurors often take considerable time in deliberation. Let me gather these papers and we can grab something to eat while we wait for the verdict."

Jesse nodded and walked to one of the tall windows, desperate for fresh air after the stifling atmosphere of the packed courtroom. The breeze felt good on his face as he gazed down at the courthouse grounds below.

His eyes caught movement - Sheriff Hayes speaking with a heavyset man in an expensive suit. The sheriff's back was to Jesse, but there was no mistaking the other man's identity. Theodore Richmond, president of Richmond Bank & Trust, stood there speaking intently with Hayes. Richmond reached out and patted the sheriff's shoulder, and Hayes immediately turned and strode away.

Jesse's stomach churned as he watched the exchange. Something about the casual familiarity between the banker and the sheriff made him deeply uneasy. The same bank foreclosing on Weber, on his family's farm, and Hayes somehow always in the middle of it all.

The jury took less than an hour to deliberate and soon filed back into the courtroom, their faces grim. Jesse studied each one as they took their seats, looking for any hint of their decision. Luke sat perfectly still, his shoulders squared and confident.

Judge White called the court to order. "All rise."

The foreman stood, unfolding a slip of paper with trembling hands. "In the case of The State of Missouri vs. John Weber, we the jury find the defendant, John W. Weber guilty on all counts."

John Weber's legs gave out and he collapsed. His wife's wail pierced the air as she fainted, slumping against family members who rushed to catch her. Angry shouts erupted throughout the courtroom.

Judge White's gavel cracked repeatedly. "Order! Order in this court!"

The crowd settled, though tension crackled through the air. Judge White adjusted his spectacles and cleared his throat. "John Weber, please rise for sentencing."

Weber's attorneys helped him to his feet. He stood there swaying, his face ashen.

"For the murder of Michael Collins, this court sentences you to twenty years in the Missouri State Penitentiary."

Mrs. Weber regained consciousness only to see deputies approaching with shackles. She lunged toward her husband but bailiffs caught her arms, holding her back as she sobbed. Weber didn't resist as they cuffed him and led him away.

Jesse turned his gaze back upon his cousin. Luke's hands trembled slightly as he shuffled his documents into his leather briefcase.

"You holdin' up alright?" Jesse asked.

Luke glanced up, his carefully maintained facade cracking for just a moment. "This part weighs heavy," he said softly. "The pronouncement of sentence. Prior proceedings are merely matters of law and evidence, but witnessing their reactions upon verdict…" He trailed off, adjusting his cufflinks.

Jesse studied his cousin. For an instant, Luke looked exactly like the boy who used to sneak extra biscuits to the neighbor's hound dog. Then Luke straightened his tie, and the polished lawyer returned.

"Weber made his choice," Luke said, voice hardening back to the prosecutor's tone. "The law remains absolute." Yet his fingers lingered over Mrs. Weber's testimony before filing it away.

"You're a mighty fine lawyer, Luke," Jesse said.

"Perhaps too proficient." Luke managed a wan smile.

8

Bad Company

The pre-dawn air felt thick in the cave's stilling chamber as Jesse helped load the last jars of moonshine. "Hauling shine in broad daylight seems about as smart as poking a hornet's nest," he said, carefully wrapping each jar in burlap.

Bill cackled, his laugh echoing off the cave walls. "That Tom, he's done got hit all figgered out - mapped ever' holler an' pig trail from here ta Kingdom Come fer dodgin' them Rev'nooers' checkpoints. Sharp as a brier, that'un."

"And if fortune turns against us?" Jesse asked.

Bill scratched his scraggly beard. "Wall, I'll tell ye what my granddaddy tolt me - iffen ye gotta dance with the devil best hope he's got hisself two left feet!" He wheezed at his own joke.

Tom's boots scraped against stone as he entered the chamber. "Ever'thing's loaded up. Had ta park the truck back a piece - too big fer bringin' down to the holler. Moved it all by wagon first-like."

Jesse nodded, knowing the steep terrain around the cave wouldn't accommodate the Atterbury. "How's she presenting?"

"Covered it proper," Tom said. "Laid down stalks of wheat an' corn overtop the shine. Casual-like glance, looks like we're jest haulin' feed."

"Better git movin' if'n we're gonna make Bolivar by meet time," Tom said, adjusting his cap.

Bill clapped them both on the shoulders. "Good luck, young'uns. Don't do nothin' I wouldn't do!" He paused, scratching his beard. "Course, that don't narrow it down none too much!"

Jesse climbed into the passenger seat as Tom cranked the engine. The truck sputtered to life, headlamps cutting through the murky dawn. As they pulled away, Jesse caught a last glimpse of Bill in the rearview, still chuckling at his own joke.

* * *

The truck rattled along the dirt road as the sun began to peek through the trees. Jesse held tight to the door handle as Tom navigated the rough terrain, the suspension groaning under the weight of their illegal cargo.

"Once't we cross the James River, we'll take them back roads till we're north of Springfield," Tom said, his eyes scanning the path ahead. "Less chance of runnin' into any trouble that-a-way."

Jesse nodded, then noticed something tucked behind the seat. Two Winchester Model 1894 .30 rifles lay across the floorboard, their wood stocks worn but well-maintained. He pulled one out, checking the action.

"Protection," Tom said before Jesse could ask. "Reckon I can set up on high ground durin' the meet with them Kansas City fellers. If somethin' goes sideways, we'll have us the 'vantage of surprise."

Jesse worked the lever of the rifle, appreciating its smooth action. The weapon brought back memories of France, where every tactical advantage could mean the difference between life and death. "Prudent thinking," he said, checking the sights one more time.

Tom smiled. "Learned me that much in the war - ain't never good ta run inta somethin' without knowin' your way back out,"

The truck bounced over a particularly rough patch, causing the moonshine jars in back to clink together. Jesse winced at the sound, but the padding they'd used seemed to be holding.

"Sounds like the cargo's holdin' steady," Tom said, reading Jesse's mind. "Old Bill taught me his packing method - said he ain't lost a jar yet on a delivery."

Jesse chuckled, "I suspect that's a load of bunk."

Tom nodded, "I reckon so too, but his way sure works better than what I was doin' before."

The sun crested over the tree line, finally giving them clear visibility of the dirt road ahead. A cloud of dust caught Jesse's eye in the side mirror - three automobiles gaining ground fast behind them.

"Got visitors," Jesse said, squinting to make out the vehicles. "Keep steady as she goes for now, but mind yourself ready."

Tom nodded, knuckles whitening on the steering wheel. "What's your play, Jesse?"

As the lead car drew closer, Jesse caught sight of a familiar face in the passenger seat - the same thug who'd worked over Virgil Coffey. "Damn. Finley River boys. Give her all she's got!"

"How'd they get wind of the shipment?" Tom yanked the throttle wide open.

"That's tomorrow's puzzle," Jesse grabbed one of the Winchesters. "Right now we're in the thick of it."

Tom glanced in the mirror. "Them's Chevrolet Series 490s - they'll do fifty-five easy. This ole truck won't break thirty, even pushin' her."

Gunfire crackled behind them. Glass shattered as bullets struck their cargo, the sharp smell of moonshine filling the air. "That's our product they're blastin' to pieces!" Tom growled.

Jesse leaned out the window, bracing the rifle against the door frame.

He squeezed off two shots at the lead car's radiator. The driver swerved, kicking up dirt. More bullets whizzed past Jesse's head as he ducked back inside.

"Hold her true!" Jesse shouted over the engine's roar. He popped back up, firing methodically. The rifle's report was sharp and clear in the morning air.

The lead car's windshield spider-webbed from one of Jesse's shots. Its driver jerked the wheel hard, nearly running off the road before recovering.

"I got an idea," Jesse called out, working the rifle's action to chamber another round. "When we hit the James River bridge, stop dead center."

Tom shot him a look like he'd lost his mind. "Ya want us ta do what now?"

"Trust me. The bridge gives us what the military calls a tactical chokepoint. Can't flank what they can't reach."

"Yeah, but we'll be sittin' ducks out here!" Tom swerved to avoid a pothole that would've rattled their cargo loose.

"So will they!" Jesse grinned.

"If'n you're wrong about this…" Tom gripped the wheel tighter.

"Mark my words - these fellows are used to easy pickings. Time they learned what two war veterans can do when properly motivated."

They turned the corner and there ahead was the bridge. The wooden planks stretched across the James River, morning mist still clinging to the water below.

"A'right, get ready - I'm fixin' ta stop. Be ready ta lay down cover fire." Tom called out, already easing off the throttle.

Jesse gripped the Winchester tighter, his finger resting alongside the trigger guard. The familiar weight of the rifle steadied his nerves. He'd been in worse spots in France, though not by much.

Tom yanked the brake lever as they hit the bridge's center. "Port side, layin' cover!" he shouted, falling into battlefield patterns. Jesse dove out his door, rifle at the ready.

"Covering you!" Jesse called back, muscle memory from the trenches taking over. The lead car screeched to a halt fifty yards back, its occupants scrambling for cover behind the doors.

"Four men, nine o'clock!" Tom's voice carried the sharp edge of combat as he crouched behind the truck's front end. His rifle cracked twice, dropping a gunman who'd tried to dash between vehicles.

Jesse's mind cleared, the world narrowing to targets and angles just like in France. "Lay down fire on that right side!" He squeezed off three rounds, forcing two men to duck behind their car's engine block.

"Got us a runner!" Tom tracked a thug trying to circle wide. His shot caught the man in the shoulder, spinning him into the ground.

The sharp ping of bullets striking metal filled the air as the gang returned fire. Jesse felt the familiar rush of adrenaline, his breathing steady as he worked the rifle's action. "Two more behind that rear motorcar!"

"I see 'em!" Tom dropped one of the men.

Jesse picked off another who'd exposed himself in the confusion. "Just like Meuse-Argonne - they bunch up when they panic!"

"These boys ain't Krauts," Tom grunted, dropping another target. "No discipline worth spit!"

Jesse checked his rifle, grimacing. "Running shy on ammo here!"

"Same," Tom called back, ducking as another bullet pinged off the truck's hood. "Down ta my last few rounds here."

Jesse squeezed off a careful shot, forcing a gunman back to cover. "Hate to say it plain, but this cargo ain't worth our final chapter."

"Agreed, but hold off a minute." Tom laid his rifle down and grabbed an old grease-stained mechanic's rag from his back pocket. He yanked open the truck's firewall panel, reaching inside the engine compartment. Something metallic clinked as he worked.

Jesse's Winchester clicked empty. "Time's up!"

"Ready!" Tom wiped his hands on the rag and stuffed something wrapped in it into his satchel. "Where to? They'll pick us off like carnival ducks if'n we run down that bridge."

"Good thing we ain't bound for that direction." Jesse peered over the bridge's edge at the James River flowing below.

Tom's eyes widened. "Ya gotta be joshin' me. You been spendin' too much time with that crazy ole coot Bill."

"Likely so," Jesse grinned, "but it's our Exodus out of here."

They scrambled onto the bridge railing as bullets sparked around them. Jesse's stomach lurched at the height - ever since falling from the hayloft as a boy, high places had turned his legs to water. But with lead in the air, fear of death outweighed fear of falling. Tom muttered a prayer before they leaped, arms pinwheeling through the air. The cool morning mist wrapped around them for a moment before they plunged into the river with twin splashes.

Jesse surfaced, spitting water. "Keep to the deep water!"

They dove beneath the surface as more shots cracked overhead, muffled by the water. The current caught them, carrying them downstream. Each time they came up for air, the bullets seemed more distant, less accurate.

Around a bend in the river, the bridge finally disappeared from view. The sounds of gunfire faded, replaced by birdsong and the gentle rush of water.

* * *

Jesse and Tom sat on the riverbank, their clothes dripping as they poured water from their boots. The morning sun had begun to warm the air, but both men still shivered from their impromptu swim.

"Can't believe we jumped off that dadgum bridge," Tom shook his head. "What in tarnation was I thinkin'?"

Jesse wrung water from his sleeve like wringing truth from a witness. "Old Thoreau had the right of it - 'The cost of a thing is the amount of life which is required to be exchanged for it.' When death comes calling, a man's got two choices - act or get planted."

"Still, that was somethin' else entirely." Tom reached for his soaked satchel. "Least I managed ta grab this here thing."

"What'd you manage to salvage from the truck?"

Tom pulled out a metal component, water dripping from its housing. "The ignition coil. They ain't gonna be able ta start that truck without it, much less drive off with it. Military trainin' comes in handy sometimes,"

Jesse chuckled despite himself. "Now that's good thinking."

"I'm awfuly sorry 'bout the shipment though," Tom's face fell. "It was our chance ta get that money fer the farm."

The reality of their situation slowly settled over Jesse. He tried to maintain his composure, but Tom clearly saw through it.

"Don't worry Jesse, we'll figure somethin' out."

"Much obliged, Tom, but-" Jesse stopped mid-sentence as a twig snapped in the distance. Both men silently moved behind large oak trees.

Jesse carefully peered around the trunk. Three men walked through the brush, carrying Springfield rifles.

"Cain't believe them crazy sumbucks jumped clean off that bridge," one said. "Ain't no way they lived through that drop."

Another man with rope coiled around his torso spoke up. "Boss wants 'em breathin'."

Jesse caught Tom's eye and used hand signals from their military days - left, right, center. Tom nodded in understanding.

Crouching down, Jesse grabbed a fist-sized rock and threw it in a high arc over the men's heads, the projectile crashing through branches thirty feet away. As they turned toward the sound, rifles raised and bodies tense, Jesse and Tom struck with practiced military precision.

They rushed forward through the underbrush - Tom taking down the man on the left with a swift tackle that knocked him cold, while Jesse charged the right man with his shoulder, driving him into a thorny blackberry bush. The impact left the second man limp and unconscious. In seconds, they had the fallen men's Springfield rifles trained on the center man, who immediately raised his calloused hands in surrender, his rope still coiled around his chest like a defeated snake.

Jesse circled the three men - now bound together around a thick oak, two slumped unconscious while the middle one remained alert - his trench knife glinting wickedly in the morning sun. "Who are you working for?" His boots crunched deliberately on fallen leaves with each step.

The conscious prisoner spat at Jesse's feet, a glob of tobacco-stained saliva darkening the dirt. "Go ta hell."

Jesse methodically wiped his blade on his sleeve, taking his time as he'd learned in the trenches that fear was often the best interrogation tool. "Reckon we'll have to carve him up proper, Tom. Shame I ain't had time to hone this blade - dull steel has an awful tendency to tear rather than slice. Makes for a mighty untidy business."

The man's face went pale as morning milk. "Hold on now! We's Finley River Gang, sure 'nuff! Jest don't start with that cuttin'!"

"That much was plain as print. Now who's writing your orders?" Jesse kept his voice casual, like they were discussing the weather.

"Feller named Bishop. Never laid eyes on 'im myself, that's the Lord's honest truth. He sends orders through other folk."

Jesse pressed the knife closer, letting the cool metal kiss the man's throat. "How'd you come by knowledge of our cargo?"

"Got us some eyes down at The Jumpin' Frog. Seen ya make that dee-livery." The man squirmed against his bonds, rope creaking. "After ya jumped our boys in town, we kept watch on yer farm, figgered you'd be movin' shine 'fore long. Warn't hard ta figure out." A nasty smile crept across his face. "Been seein' that pretty blonde girl workin' the fields too."

Tom lunged forward, his face dark with rage. "You been watchin' Mary?" His fist connected with the man's jaw before Jesse could move.

Jesse grabbed Tom's shoulder, pulling him back with one hand while pressing the other against his chest. Their eyes met – Jesse's steady gaze a silent command to let him handle this. Tom's jaw worked as he stepped back, his hands still clenched into fists, but he nodded once.

Jesse's own jaw clenched at the mention of them watching his property, his mind flashing to Mary and his mother. "Who's the outfit you're steering clear of? The ones with real muscle?"

"Don't know nothin' 'bout that. I's jest small taters." Sweat beaded on the man's forehead as he worked his bruised jaw, turning his head to spit a stream of crimson onto the dirt. The blood mixed with saliva, and he ran his tongue over his teeth, checking for loose ones. The red spatter seemed to please Tom, who still stood rigid, his hands still balled into fists at his sides.

Jesse reached into his pocket and pulled out a Cherry Chaser candy, one that he had bought at Halloway's. "Ever read about them brown bears in these hills? Their sense of smell's keener than a preacher's conscience - two miles out, they can catch a whiff." He unwrapped it slow as reading verse. "And cherries? Why, drives 'em mad with hunger."

"Ye can't-"

"Can't?" Jesse crushed the candy between his fingers and dropped it just out of reach, the sweet scent filling the air. "Seems to me you forgot you and your boys tried turning that bridge into our own private theater of war." He pulled the man's handkerchief free, converting it to a gag that silenced the man's rising terror. "Now you're about to learn what Prometheus felt like, bound and waiting for something hungry to arrive."

"Best we move along, Tom." Jesse grabbed the Springfield rifles, appreciating their familiar weight as he slung them over his shoulder, and headed toward their abandoned truck.

After they'd put some distance between them, Tom spoke up, scratching his stubbled chin. "You know that thing about brown bears ain't true, right?"

Jesse grinned, "I know that. But he doesn't."

*　*　*

Jesse and Tom made their way back to the bridge, finding their truck exactly where they'd left it. The wheat and corn that had concealed their moonshine cargo lay scattered across the wooden planks like fallen soldiers, and every jar of shine was gone. Save those that shattered in the gunfight, remnants of glass shards and moonshine lay sprawled across the truck bed.

"Well, your quick thinking saved us that ignition coil at least," Jesse said, running his hand along the truck's battle-scarred hood. "Reckon the old girl's still got some fight left in her, damaged as she is."

Tom leaned against the vehicle's side, wiping sweat from his brow. "What's the play here? We goin' after them Finley River boys?"

Jesse shook his head, holding up one of the captured Springfield rifles. "These are Army issue - same breed we carried through the mud of France. Man doesn't maintain weapons like this unless he's got a whole arsenal tucked away somewhere." He checked the rifle's action, finding it smooth and well-maintained. "Two men against their whole outfit - those odds aren't in our favor."

"So we jest gonna let 'em walk away after what they done?" Tom's voice carried a hint of frustration.

"For the present moment," Jesse said, watching Tom work the ignition coil back into position. "Let's get this heart back in her chest and make for home. Bank's clock's ticking down - ten days before they come calling. Need to devise ourselves another strategy for keeping the farm."

9

Desperate Times

Jesse sat in a rickety old chair, its joints creaking with every slight movement, watching Bill clean his copper stills. The limestone cave chamber held the familiar sweet-sour smell of corn mash as the old moonshiner scrubbed and polished the equipment, his gnarled hands moving with surprising grace over each piece.

"You young'uns is lucky ta still be drawin' breath," Bill said, scrubbing hard at a stubborn spot of residue inside the copper pot. "Them Finley River boys ain't known fer lettin' folk walk away breathin'. Done seen 'em gut men like field hogs fer less'n what you done to their bunch. Yes sir, seen it with these two eyes, I have."

"Rose needs warning about that Judas at The Jumping Frog," Jesse replied, absently running his thumb along the worn silver case of his father's pocket watch. The timepiece's familiar weight had become both comfort and burden since his father's death - each tick now seemed to count down both precious memories and the few days they had left to save the family land.

"Fixin' ta head up that-a-way come tomorrow night." Bill wiped down the copper coil with a well-worn rag, his remaining fingers working methodically. "But we gotta be slicker'n a greased pig about it. Spook that rat and they'll scatter faster'n cockroaches when ya light lamp."

Jesse nodded, his mind working through the possibilities. "Them fellers ya'll strung up down by the river - reckon anybody done found their sorry hides by now?" Asked Bill as he plugged tobacco into his cheek. "Them water moccasins get mighty curious 'bout things tied up near their swimmin' holes, they do."

"Them knots are tight as sin - take a sharp blade to undo 'em," Jesse said, remembering the satisfaction of securing the rope. "Only way they're loose is if their compatriots came calling with steel."

"That yapper what spilled his guts - ya reckon he'll keep his trap shut 'bout singin' like a jaybird?" Bill spat a stream of tobacco juice. "Them kind's got 'bout as much loyalty as a barn cat in heat. Liable ta switch masters quick as lightnin' if'n they think it'll save their hide."

"If there's sense in his head, he surely will. In outfits like that, a loose tongue gets you killed faster than failing." Jesse leaned back in his chair, wincing as it threatened to give way. "Reckon he'll keep mum if he's partial to drawing breath."

"Ya'll got too much faith in them peckerwoods," Bill said, shaking his head as he polished a copper pipe. "Done seen more'n my share turn yeller'n a summer squash when the squeezin' starts."

"Maybe so." Jesse sighed, feeling the weight of their situation. "Right now my thoughts are fixed on that twenty-five hundred we're shy. Richmond's circling our farm like them Turkey buzzards- patient-like, knowing their dinner ain't got nowhere to run."

The sound of running footsteps echoed through the cave passage, bouncing off the rocky walls. Tom burst into the chamber, out of breath, his face red with exertion and worry.

"Jesse! Ya need ta come quick - Richmond's men is at the farmhouse!"

* * *

Jesse and Tom galloped hard toward the farmhouse, their horses' hooves thundering against the dusty dirt. As they approached, Jesse could see a cluster of men gathered in the yard - a well-dressed man in a tailored suit stood front and center, Deputy Cole shifting nervously beside him, and four or five others in cheaper business attire hanging back, clutching clipboards and surveying the property. Above it all, Mary's voice rose sharp and clear.

"Ya ain't got no right bein' here!" Mary shouted, her face flushed with anger as she confronted the man in the suit. "This here's private property, and ya'll are trespassin'!" Mary glanced at Deputy Cole, hoping he would step in.

Deputy William Cole stood awkwardly to the side, shifting his weight from foot to foot, his badge gleaming in the afternoon sun. He kept his eyes fixed on his scuffed boots, unable or unwilling to meet Jesse's steady gaze.

"P-please, Miz Walker," Cole stammered, studying a patch of dirt near his feet, "I's jest here ta keep the peace is all. Cain't go interferin' with no bank business, no ma'am."

Sarah leaned against the porch column, her knuckles white as she gripped the weathered wood. Jesse's heart tightened at the sight of his mother's distress.

Jesse dismounted in one fluid motion, his boots hitting the ground hard as he strode toward the men. "What's the meaning of this?" he demanded, his voice carrying the authority he'd learned commanding men in France.

The man adjusted his round wire-rimmed glasses, consulting a leather portfolio. "Are you Jesse Walker?"

"I am."

"Clarence Milton, Richmond Bank & Trust." He extended a document toward Jesse with a practiced motion. "We're here to begin inventory of farm equipment for upcoming auction."

Jesse snatched the paper, scanning its contents quickly. "This is absurd. Our time ain't run its course on that final payment."

Milton's thin lips curved into what might have been a smile. "If you'll review the contract your father signed, you'll see that ten days prior to default, the bank has full rights to begin preparation for equipment auction. It's all quite legal, I assure you."

"Ya'll cain't do this!" Mary's face contorted with rage and her rough hands balled into fists. "This here equipment belongs ta us - we done paid fer it with our sweat and our blood! Every last piece was bought fair and square with Walker money!"

"Mary," Jesse warned, his voice low and controlled. "This ain't helping."

"Helpin'?" She whirled on him, eyes flashing. "Standin' there while they steal ever'thing we own ain't helpin' neither!"

Jesse caught Tom's eye with a subtle glance. Tom nodded, understanding the silent request.

"Come on now, Mary," Tom said gently, placing a hand on her shoulder. "Let's us take a walk. Ain't no good gonna come from this right now."

"Don't you dare touch me!" But her voice cracked as Tom carefully guided her away from the scene.

Jesse turned back to Milton, his jaw clenched. "Do what you reckon you must, then - but remember what the Good Book says about reaping what you sow."

Jesse watched, his anger simmering beneath a carefully controlled exterior, as Milton signaled his men to begin their work. The repo men scattered across the farm like vultures, clipboards in hand, methodically documenting everything of value.

"Rumely OilPull, 1911 model," one called out, circling the tractor Tom had recently repaired. "Needs work but should fetch three hundred at auction."

Another man ran his hands along the plow, testing its edge. "Good steel here, barely worn. Add it to the list."

They moved through the barn, examining the horses with cold efficiency. "These two could pull their weight in a logging operation," one commented, pointing to Jesse's mare and Mary's gelding. "Market's good for draft horses right now."

Milton stood in the yard, orchestrating the inventory like a conductor, making notes in his leather portfolio as his men called out items and values.

The repo men poked through every corner of the property, marking down tools, equipment, even the hand-cranked corn sheller Jesse's grandfather had built. They discussed potential buyers and auction estimates as if the Walker family weren't even present, their voices carrying across the yard with casual indifference.

Like ants swarming over fallen fruit, they methodically stripped away the dignity of everything the Walkers had built, reducing it all to numbers in a ledger. After what felt like hours but couldn't have been more than forty-five minutes, Milton closed his portfolio with a sharp snap.

He and his men loaded into their automobiles without a backward glance, leaving only dust and the echo of their callous appraisals behind.

Jesse turned toward the house. Mary sat on the porch steps sobbing while Tom awkwardly patted her shoulder. Sarah stood motionless, her face ashen.

Suddenly, Sarah's eyes rolled back and she crumpled to the ground.

"Mamma!" Jesse bolted forward as she collapsed. Tom was already moving, helping Jesse reach her side.

"Got to get her to her bed," Jesse said urgently. He looked at Tom. "Fetch Doc Wilson - ride fast as you can!"

Tom was already running for his horse before Jesse finished speaking.

* * *

Jesse sat rigid in his father's old leather chair, puffing mechanically on his pipe as he stared through the open window. The sweet scent of tobacco did little to calm his churning thoughts. Mary perched on the edge of the settee, fingers twisting her apron while Tom stood near the doorway.

The sharp click of the bedroom door cut through the silence. All three rose in unison as Doc Wilson's weathered form appeared in the sitting room doorway, his black medical bag clutched in one hand.

"What ails her, Doc?" Jesse asked, pipe forgotten in his hand.

"Mo' than likely what we're lookin' at here is a case of Heart Shock," Doctor Wilson removed his wire-rimmed spectacles, wiping them with his monogrammed handkerchief. "Brought on by extreme stress, you understand. These tryin' times can be particularly hard on a lady of Mrs. Walker's gentle disposition. The shock of today's… unpleasantness… well." He cleared his throat delicately.

"Will she recover?" Jesse's voice carried an edge of desperation.

"She'll recover," the doctor said, replacing his glasses. "However, I must caution you - any mo' disturbances of this nature may prove too taxin' on her heart. I recommend two teaspoons of valerian tincture in water, mornin' and night." He paused, patting his vest pocket for his prescription pad. "And bed rest, that's absolutely essential, you understand. Complete peace and quiet - no upset whatsoever. Perhaps…" he hesitated diplomatically, "perhaps it might be prudent to keep any further… business matters… away from the house entirely."

Jesse and Mary exchanged glances before nodding. "We'll make sure she gets it, and we'll follow ever' last one of your orders, Doctor Wilson." Mary assured him.

"Much obliged for your haste, Doctor," Jesse said, walking the physician to the door. "Means more than words can properly express."

"Of course, of course," Doctor Wilson replied, picking up his hat. "Do send word if there's any change in her condition."

After the doctor left, Jesse slumped back into his father's chair, the weight of everything pressing down on his shoulders.

"Mary, keep watch over Mama," Jesse said, his voice rough with emotion.

"What're ya fixin' to do?" Mary asked, still fidgeting with her apron.

Jesse ran a hand through his hair. "Can't rightly say. The fault lies at my feet. If I'd found our way clear of this mess sooner, Mama wouldn't be laid low."

"That ain't true and you know it!" Mary shot back. "You're workin' yourself to the bone tryin' to save this farm. We all see it - up before dawn, home after dark. Even Tom says he ain't never seen nobody work as hard as you do, and that man knows what real work looks like."

"Fat lot of good that's accomplished." Jesse stood up abruptly. "My best effort's proved about as useful as a glass hammer. Bank's fixing to strip us bare as Job, and now Mama's took sick on account of my shortcomings."

He strode out of the sitting room, the screen door banging behind him. Tom followed silently, giving Jesse space as he paced the worn boards of the porch. The evening air was thick with humidity, matching the heaviness in Jesse's chest.

After wearing a path in the floorboards, Jesse turned to Tom. "Make tracks to Bill's - tell him we're calling on Rose tonight. Best get that boat ready."

Tom nodded, understanding in his eyes, and headed toward the cave without another word.

* * *

The muffled sound of a piano drifted through the heavy summer night

113

as Jesse, Bill, and Tom made their way up the narrow path to The Jumping Frog. Laughter and the clink of glasses filtered through the cave walls, mixing with chirping crickets and rustling leaves in the oak trees overhead. The path wound between weathered outcroppings until they reached the wooden facade covering the cave entrance, its planks worn smooth by countless patrons' hands.

A large Native American man stood guard, his broad shoulders blocking the doorway like a living wall. His dark eyes, sharp as obsidian, studied them carefully as they approached, lingering on Jesse's military bearing and Bill's eccentric appearance. The guard's hand rested casually near his holstered revolver.

"Password?" he asked, his deep voice barely above a whisper, carried on the night breeze.

"Langhorne," Jesse replied, meeting the man's gaze steadily.

The guard nodded, his expression unchanging. "You may pass."

"Hold fast," Jesse said, holding up a calloused hand. "We need words with Rose - private-like. Can you fetch her out here?"

"Not possible," the guard stated flatly, his boots planted firmly on the packed earth.

"Matter's urgent. "Seems you've got yourself a Judas in The Jumping Frog." Jesse explained, keeping his voice low but urgent.

The guard's stoic expression cracked for a moment, showing surprise in the slight widening of his eyes. He turned and knocked three sharp raps on the wooden door, the sound echoing off the cave walls. Another Native American man, shorter but equally broad, opened it slightly, and the two exchanged rapid words in Osage, their ancient language flowing like water. The man inside shook his head before closing the door firmly.

Moments later Rose emerged from the entrance, her elegant dress a stark contrast to the rough cave walls. "Mes amis," she said, "this better not be a joke."

"It's not," Jesse replied. "Finley River boys laid a trap for us yesterday near James River bridge. One of their men, after some persuading, spoke of having eyes inside your establishment."

"One of my people?" Rose asked sharply.

"Don't reckon so," Jesse said, shaking his head. "Call to mind them fellows who worked over Virgil? They were hunting information from someone close to your operation. Way I figure it - it's more likely a regular patron than your people. Someone watching with purpose."

Rose's expression darkened. "Someone who watches more than he drinks…"

"Indeed," Jesse nodded. "A body careful to keep his wits while others lose theirs."

"Duffy," Rose said decisively. "Regular as sunrise, but careful with his drink. Now that my mind turns to it - when did you say this… unfortunate event occurred?"

"Yesterday."

A knowing smile crossed Rose's face. "Mais oui, how interesting. Duffy wasn't here yesterday. In fact, I've noticed his empty chair matches perfect with every hit on our fellow operators."

"Sounds like our man," Jesse agreed.

Rose turned to her Osage guards and spoke rapidly in their native tongue. They nodded grimly and melted away into the darkness. She turned back to Jesse and the others.

"This way, gentlemen," she said, holding the door open. "Let's settle this matter properly."

Inside The Jumping Frog, a ragtime tune filled the chamber as patrons crowded around tables, their laughter mixing with the clink of glass and shuffle of cards. Smoke from cigars and cigarettes drifted up toward the limestone ceiling, creating a hazy veil above the revelry.

Rose strode in with purpose, her Osage guards flanking her like shadows. Jesse spotted Duffy in the corner, his eyes darting between the bar and the crowd while pretending to sip from a glass that never seemed to empty.

In one fluid motion, Rose drew a nickel-plated revolver and fired into the cave ceiling. The sharp crack echoed through the chamber, silencing the piano and freezing every patron mid-motion.

"My deepest apologies, chers clients," Rose announced, her voice carrying authority despite its sweetness. "We must close early tonight. Some private affairs require attention."

The crowd moved quickly and quietly toward the exit, no one daring to question Rose's orders. As Duffy tried to blend in with the departing patrons, one of the Osage men stepped into his path, blocking his escape.

"Non," Rose said, her eyes fixed on Duffy. "You'll stay right where you are."

Panic flashed across Duffy's face. He spun toward the exit, as he shoved a chair between himself and the approaching guards, sending it clattering across the floor.

"Now, now," Rose's voice cut through the tension like a knife. "Is that any way to treat my hospitality? After all these months of keeping my chairs warm and my secrets cold?"

Duffy reached for something under his coat, but the guards were faster. The first caught his arm while the second drove a shoulder into his gut, sending all three crashing into a nearby table. Cards and chips scattered across the floor as they struggled. Despite his desperate thrashing, Duffy was no match for the Osage warriors.

They pinned him face-down on the wooden planks, his cheek pressed against spilled liquor and scattered playing cards. The Queen of Hearts stared back at him, as merciless as Rose's gaze.

"You know," Rose said, examining her revolver with casual interest, "my people have ancient ways of dealing with those who betray trust. Ways that make your employers seem… comment dit-on… gentle by comparison."

The guards dragged Duffy down a dark passageway, his boots scraping against the stone floor. His screams echoed off the cave walls until they faded into silence. Rose turned to Jesse, Bill, and Tom with a warm smile that didn't quite reach her eyes.

"Now then, mes amis - shall we share a drink? On the house, of course."

***

Rose reached for a bottle of amber liquid and poured three fingers each into heavy glass tumblers. The whiskey caught the lantern light as she slid them across the bar to Jesse and Bill. She offered one to Tom, who stared at it for a long moment, his fingers twitching slightly before he pushed it away.

"Water, if you don't mind, Miss Rose," he said quietly, his voice rough.

Rose's expression softened with understanding as she replaced the whiskey with a glass of clear spring water. A muffled scream echoed from deep within the cave passages.

"I can't thank you boys enough," Rose said, her fingers drumming against the bar top. "That serpent Duffy, sitting here night after night, watching like a hawk circling prey." Her face darkened with anger. "Some suppliers never darkened my door, but the ones who did..." She shook her head. "The Finley River Gang made sure their stills went cold."

Jesse stared into his glass, lost in thought, before throwing back the whiskey in one swift motion. The liquor burned, but he barely noticed.

"That thar shipment woulda done it right proper," Bill said, his voice heavy with regret. "Woulda give Jesse 'nuff scratch ta save that Walker place, shore 'nuff." He spat a stream of tobacco juice into a nearby spittoon. "Now that fancy-britches Richmond's gonna own it in ten days, less'n sumthin' changes right quick."

Jesse pushed his empty glass toward Rose. "Pour another, if you'd be so kind."

She grabbed the bottle and poured, watching as Jesse immediately downed the second glass, his eyes fixed on some distant point only he could see.

"Word has it you're something of an information broker. I find myself in need of certain… intelligence." Said Jesse.

Rose leaned forward across the bar, her dark eyes studying Jesse intently. "What exactly are you proposing, cher?"

"Richmond Bank & Trust. Their St. Louis money transfers - timing and method."

"Boy, you done lost what little sense th' Good Lawd done give ya!" Bill cackled, slapping the bar top. "Though I gotta say, this here kinda crazy fits ya jest fine."

Rose's fingers tightened around the whiskey bottle. "Mon Dieu, that's dancing with the devil himself, Jesse. Richmond's got the Romano family from St. Louis behind them, strong as an oak tree's roots. They'll hunt you through hell's half acre if you touch their money."

"That bank's been picking our bones clean for years now," Jesse's voice was cold steel. "Figure it's high time they learned what it feels like to be on the receiving end. And I aim to be right charitable about it - use their own money to square our debt."

"Hot damn!" Bill whooped. "Count me in on this here foolishness! Been too long since I had me some real fun!" His toothless grin spread wide beneath his scraggly beard.

Jesse turned to Tom. "This here's a different kind of battle than what you bargained for. Ain't asking you to carry this weight."

Tom straightened, meeting Jesse's gaze. "Since I met you and yours, I finally got control of the drinkin'. First time since France I feel like…" he paused, searching for the right words, "like I'm part of somethin' that matters again. Haven't had that since leaving the Three-Five." His calloused hands clenched briefly at his sides. "I'm in, Sarge. All the way in."

Rose shook her head, but a slight smile played at her lips. "You're either blessed with courage or cursed with foolishness, Jesse Walker." She reached across the bar, her fingers brushing his as she took his empty glass. "Hopefully the former. My people will find what you need. Consider it fair exchange for catching our rat."

"Much obliged," Jesse said softly, holding her gaze a moment longer than necessary. The lantern light played across her raven-black hair, and for a moment he forgot about banks and mobs and failing farms.

"Don't sing victory yet, cher," Rose said, but her eyes held a warmth that betrayed her stern tone. "Truth can bite harder than any snake."

Tom glanced at Bill and nodded toward the card tables. "Think I see an empty seat over there."

"Reckon my luck's bound ta turn," Bill cackled, pushing away from the bar with surprising agility for his age. His ancient boots scraped against the wooden floor. "Last time I only lost my boots an' dignity. Still got my shirt though, praise th' Lawd fer small mercies."

Jesse watched them leave before turning back to Rose. She was polishing a glass with practiced efficiency, but her movements seemed more deliberate than necessary. The lamplight caught the smooth curve of her cheekbone as she worked, her eyes focused intently on the task.

"Your father," Rose said softly, memories mellowing her accent. "Last summer, when my well ran dry, he brought water up here every day for near two weeks. Wouldn't take a dime for it neither."

"Sounds like him," Jesse said, memories of his father's quiet generosity washing over him. "Father never could abide seeing folks in need. Even when our own table was mighty lean, he'd find something to share. Mama used to say he had a heart bigger than his common sense."

Rose's hand found his on the bar top, her skin surprisingly soft despite her work. "You carry his spirit, same fire burning behind those eyes when someone needs help."

Jesse felt the warmth of her touch spread up his arm. "Can't say I'm certain about that. Father always knew right from wrong - nowadays seems like the compass needle's spinning wild."

"This world's gone wild as a spring storm," Rose said, her fingers drawing symbols on his palm. "Good men bend like willows or break like oak. Your daddy knew that truth.""

Jesse looked up, meeting her gaze. The lantern light danced in her dark eyes, highlighting flecks of amber he'd never noticed before, and he found himself leaning closer. "And what about good women, Miss Rose?"

"We learn to survive," she whispered, her breath warm as summer wind. "Sometimes we trust those others fear. Sometimes we see light where others find shadow."

"Is that what we're building here?" Jesse asked, his voice low, rough with emotion he couldn't quite name. "Something like trust?"

Rose pulled back slightly, but her hand remained on his, her touch both comfort and torment. "I can't name what this is between us, Jesse Walker. And that's what excites me."

10

The Last Car

Jesse traced his finger along the worn map spread across the truck's hood, the paper crackling in the hot Missouri wind. Highway 60 stretched empty before them, the afternoon sun beating down mercilessly.

"One chance at this play," he said, tapping a spot where railroad tracks snaked beneath a small cliff. "We drop when the train passes beneath. One misstep…" He let the words hang in the air. "Then we make our way aft - Rose's intelligence confirms the bank keeps their money in a private car, hitched on the tail end of the caboose like a tick on a hound."

Tom shifted his weight, adjusting the rifle strap across his shoulder. "How do we handle their muscle?"

Jesse reached into his satchel, pulling out two metal canisters. The military-grade smoke grenades felt heavy in his palm, familiar yet strange so far from the trenches of France. "Rose procured these somehow."

"Just like what we used overseas," Tom said, examining one with practiced hands. "Makes ya wonder what else that woman's got hidden away. Rose ain't exactly your typical speakeasy owner, that's fer certain."

"I pity those who make her their enemy," Jesse muttered, returning to the map. His finger traced a thin line representing a service road. "Bill, here's your piece of the puzzle. Bring that truck down this trail and meet us precise at this spot. We've got to unhitch that rear car and be stopped dead - miss it, and we're stranded in the worst kind of backcountry. Won't be no reaching us in time."

Jesse looked up at his companions. "Next stop's Rolla - should give us breathing room enough to fade away before they can muster their forces. Everyone's mind clear on this?"

Bill and Tom nodded solemnly.

"Three-quarters of an hour till our train shows," Jesse said, folding the map. "Best get ourselves set. And Tom - them guns - last resort when nothing else serves. If we can write this tale without bloodshed, so much the better."

Tom gave a curt nod, his expression grim but determined.

* * *

Jesse peered over the small cliff's edge at the railroad tracks below, his stomach tightening at the drop. It was further down than he'd anticipated, and heights had never been his friend.

Tom stood beside him, looking down before letting out a nervous chuckle. "Piece of cake."

Jesse glanced at his companion, both worried and amused by the false bravado. Reaching into his vest pocket, he retrieved his tobacco tin, the initials 'JW' catching the sunlight as he pulled it out. With practiced motions, he packed his pipe, hoping the familiar ritual would settle his nerves.

"You know," Tom said, shifting his weight back from the edge, "I've run across no man's land many a time, and yet I think I feel more nervous right now than that."

"Makes about as much sense as a summer snowfall," Jesse agreed, drawing on his pipe. "Running through them fields in France with German lead singing overhead…" He shook his head, smoke curling around him like memory's ghost. "Reckon peace made us soft - strange how a man can get used to hell itself, then find his nerves jangling at its echo."

Tom nodded solemnly. "Sounds reasonable."

Their contemplation was cut short by a train horn echoing in the distance. Jesse quickly tapped out his pipe, tucking it into his satchel and returning the tobacco tin to his vest pocket.

Jesse and Tom lay down on the cliffside waiting. Over the horizon, black smoke gradually appeared in the distance, the train chugging up the hill at a fraction of its normal speed - exactly why Jesse had chosen this spot. The locomotive grew louder as it approached, its smokestack belching thick dark clouds.

Jesse and Tom stood, Winchester repeaters strapped to their backs and revolvers on their hips, tensed for the jump.

"Jump!" Jesse yelled. Without hesitation, they leaped from the cliff, hard onto the roof of the freight car. Tom overshot and began sliding off the edge, fingers desperately grasping for something to cling to. Jesse lunged forward and caught Tom's hands just in time, his companion's body dangling precariously off the side of the moving train.

With straining muscles, Jesse slowly pulled Tom back up. They rolled over, gasping for breath, the wind whipping past them. Tom clutched his chest, still panting.

"Thanks," he managed.

Jesse, eyes wide from the close call, replied, "Don't mention it."

They crept forward across the roof, carefully making their way over three more freight cars, their boots finding careful traction on the metal surfaces. The steady chug of the locomotive masked their movement as they passed above cargo destined for St. Louis. Finally, they reached the coupling that connected the last freight car to the caboose. Descending the ladder between cars, Jesse pressed himself against the wall, peering through the grimy window.

"See anythin'?" Tom whispered.

"Can't rightly see much - windows are too hazy." Jesse pulled his black mask over his face. "We should be clear. Let's go."

Tom followed suit with his mask and yanked open the door. They burst inside only to freeze - three men sat waiting, two holding shotguns while a third clutched a Thompson submachine gun.

A shotgun blast tore through the air, splintering the wooden wall inches from Jesse's head. The acrid smell of gunpowder filled the confined space as Jesse dove right and Tom went left.

A mobster swung his shotgun like a club, but Jesse ducked and drove his shoulder into the man's gut. The tommy gunner tried to bring his weapon around but Tom tackled him, sending the gun clattering across the floor.

The third man pulled a knife, slashing at Jesse. The blade caught his vest, tearing the fabric. Jesse trapped the man's knife arm and delivered a sharp elbow to his jaw. The mobster staggered but kept his grip on the blade.

Tom grappled with his opponent, their bodies crashing into the walls. Jesse's attacker lunged again with the knife. This time Jesse caught the thrust, twisted the man's wrist and slammed his head into a support beam. The mobster crumpled.

The first gunman had regained his feet but Tom's opponent flew backwards into him, courtesy of a powerful shove. Both men went down in a tangle. Jesse and Tom pounced, delivering precise strikes until all three mobsters lay unconscious.

Breathing hard, Jesse retrieved the tommy gun while Tom efficiently unloaded the shotguns. With a metallic click, Tom locked the front door of the caboose.

After securing the unconscious mobsters, they moved to the connecting door between the caboose and the private car ahead. Through the window, Jesse could see the car's luxurious interior – leather seats, polished wood panels, and at the rear, a massive Mosler bank safe. The black iron vault stood about four feet tall and three feet wide, its brass combination dial catching the dim light. Five armed men surrounded it, two with Tommy guns and three with revolvers.

"Five more up ahead," Jesse whispered. "Looking mighty serious about their business."

"You sure this time?" Tom asked, a hint of skepticism in his voice.

Jesse shot him a pointed look through his mask.

Standing up straight, Jesse grabbed his smoke grenade. "Ready with yours?" At Tom's nod, he yanked the pin and flung open the door. The grenade sailed inside before Jesse slammed it shut again.

Shouts and coughs erupted from within as thick gray smoke filled the car. The door handle rattled violently.

"Let us out!" voices yelled through fits of coughing.

"Now!" Jesse called to Tom, who threw open the caboose door.

Jesse yanked open the private end car's door. Mobsters stumbled out, eyes streaming, lunging blindly toward the caboose. Jesse shoved the last man through just as Tom unpinned his grenade and tossed it in, unleashing another choking cloud. Tom slammed the door, wedging one of the captured shotguns through the handle.

Jesse ducked into the now-empty private car while Tom worked the coupling mechanism. Metal screeched against metal as the car broke free, gradually falling behind as the train continued forward with its cargo of smoke-blind mobsters.

"Need them brakes hit hard," Jesse called from the doorway. "Our rendevous is comin' quick."

Tom cranked the private car's brake wheel as it screamed against the rails, throwing sparks until they shuddered to a stop.

Through the settling dust, Jesse spotted Bill driving the truck down the service road right on schedule. The old man brought the vehicle alongside the car's door while Jesse and Tom worked to free the safe from its moorings.

"This thing weighs more than a tank," Tom grunted as they finally unbolted it. Sweat dripped down their faces as they strained against the safe's bulk, slowly inching the iron beast toward the door.

With a final heave, Jesse and Tom managed to slide the safe onto the truck bed, the vehicle's suspension groaning under the weight.

Tom quickly threw a tarp over the safe while Jesse gathered the weapons, concealing them beneath the cover. They jumped into the truck as Bill gunned the engine, the tires spinning briefly before finding drag on the dusty road.

They bumped along the service road heading back toward Lebanon, the safe's weight making the truck's rear end sag. Jesse kept watch out the back window, but saw no signs of pursuit yet. The train's whistle echoed in the distance, growing fainter as they put miles between themselves and their handiwork.

* * *

The truck rumbled down the dirt path leading to the Walker Farm as the sun began it's decent over the horizon. Jesse's heart still raced from their train heist as Bill carefully backed the truck as close as they could to the cave.

"Easy does it," Jesse called as they maneuvered the heavy safe from the truck bed. The metal groaned as they lowered it onto a makeshift dolly Tom had constructed from old wagon wheels.

Inside the cave's main chamber, the smell of Bill's latest batch of moonshine mixed with the musty cave air as they positioned the safe.

"What if'n that box is empty as a preacher's liquor cabinet?" Bill pondered, working his fingers through his tangled beard.

Jesse and Tom turned to him simultaneously. "Best not tempt fate with such talk," Jesse warned.

Tom pulled a hand drill from his toolbag and positioned it against the safe's lock mechanism. "Only one way to find out. Help me lay her on her back."

Jesse and Bill tipped the safe carefully, the metal scraping against the cave floor. Tom began working the drill, the grinding sound echoing through the chamber as metal shavings fell to the ground.

"Slower," Jesse advised, hovering over Tom's shoulder. "Don't want to damage anything inside."

Bill paced nervously, muttering something about "Guv'ment men" under his breath. The minutes stretched on as Tom methodically worked the drill through the lock's tumblers.

Finally, after what felt like hours, there was a distinctive click. Tom sat back on his heels, wiping sweat from his brow. "That should do it."

With trembling hands, Tom grasped the safe's handle and turned it. The heavy door swung open with a low creak.

Jesse knelt beside the open safe, his heart pounding as he reached inside. His eyes widened as he pulled out stack after stack of crisp bills. The musty cave air felt electric with possibility.

"Lord above," Jesse breathed, laying out the stacks in neat rows. "Must be north of twenty-five thousand here - more money than I've ever seen in my life."

Bill let out a low whistle while Tom stood speechless, staring at the small fortune spread before them. The lantern light made the money seem to glow against the dark limestone.

"Seems mighty strange to move this much cash at once," Tom said, finally finding his voice. He picked up one of the stacks, turning it over in his hands. "This don't appear to be a normal money transfer."

"You speak truth," Jesse said. "This arithmetic don't balance proper."

Bill stopped pacing and planted himself in front of them. "Listen hyar, we gotta be cunnin' as them hill foxes 'bout this whole thang," Bill said, tugging at his beard. "Take whut's needed fer savin' the farm, then we'll plant the rest of them greenbacks so deep in these hyar caves that the Good Lawd Hisself'd need him a map ta find 'em." He gestured toward the darker recesses of the chamber. "I'll make that iron box vanish faster'n a lightnin' bug in a thunderstorm."

Jesse nodded slowly. "You both risked hide and happiness helping me with this venture. Ain't got words proper enough to express my gratitude."

Bill waved him off. "Hell, I'd kidnap the guv'nor's wife iffen it meant keepin' my still flowin'," he cackled.

"There's still one problem," Tom said. "How're you gonna explain suddenly havin' the money to your mother and Mary?"

Jesse ran a hand through his hair. "Been thinking on that. Need to come up with something that won't raise questions - something simple enough to believe, but not so simple it falls apart under looking at."

* * *

Jesse and Tom trudged up the path from the cave, their boots heavy with exhaustion, muscles aching from the day's labor. The sight of Luke's shiny Model T parked in front of the weathered farmhouse made Jesse pause momentarily.

Inside, the welcoming aroma of Sarah's cooking - fresh baked bread and what smelled like beef stew - filled the air. Luke rose smoothly from his chair, carefully folded newspaper in hand. "Cousin Jesse, I came by to check on everyone after that unpleasantness the other day," he said.

"Truth be told, I'm doing finer than a spring morning," Jesse said, his voice carrying through the house like a dinner bell. The military authority he'd learned overseas naturally crept into his tone. "Might everyone gather in the sitting room? Got something worth hearing."

Mary appeared from the kitchen, wiping flour from her calloused hands, followed by Sarah who methodically wiped her hands on her worn but spotless apron. They gathered around as Jesse reached into his coat and pulled out a thick stack of bills.

"Three thousand and five hundred dollars," he announced, holding up the money like a trophy. "Enough to square our debt with Richmond's bank."

Sarah's weathered hand flew to her mouth while Mary gasped, her eyes wide as saucers. Luke's eyes widened too, his smile faltering for just a moment.

"How… where'd this come from?" Mary stammered, her voice trembling with hope and disbelief.

Jesse cleared his throat, the lie coming easier than he'd expected. "Was going through Father's old workshop, out in the barn. Found it tucked away in an old tin pail, hidden behind his tools. Must've been his hedge against hard times."

"Oh, thank the Lord," Sarah whispered, tears streaming down her lined face as she embraced Jesse, her thin frame shaking with emotion.

Mary launched herself at Tom, wrapping him in an excited hug that caught the veteran off guard. "We get to keep the farm!" she exclaimed, her joy infectious enough to bring a smile to Tom's face.

"I'll ride into town come day after tomorrow, set things proper with the bank," Jesse said.

Luke lingered after Sarah and Mary returned to the kitchen, their excited chatter drifting through the house. He studied Jesse with careful eyes.

"Well now, that's quite a stroke of luck, finding that money," Luke said, his lawyer's practiced tone probing. "Interesting timing, wouldn't you say?"

Jesse met his cousin's gaze steadily. "Father always did have a knack for planning ahead."

"Yes, he did," Luke agreed, folding his newspaper with precise movements. "Though it does make you wonder why he'd keep that kind of money in a tin can while the bank was breathing down his neck."

"Age has a way of making even sharp minds forget things," Jesse said, keeping his voice balanced. "Could be he was saving it for when things got truly desperate, hoping he'd never need to use it at all."

Luke nodded slowly, his eyes never leaving Jesse's face. "Well, I'm glad it worked out for you all. Better head back - got a stack of papers waiting." He paused at the door. "Give my best to Aunt Sarah."

After Luke's automobile disappeared down the drive, Tom joined Jesse on the porch. They watched the sunset paint the cornfields gold.

"Think they bought it?" Tom asked quietly.

Jesse gazed at the horizon where the sun was sinking into a bed of orange and purple clouds. "Won't matter much if they do. By the time questions start flying, that debt'll be cleared clean as a new slate and the farm'll be anchored safely." Tom nodded silently as the twilight deepened around them, crickets beginning their evening chorus across the darkening fields.

11

The Gathering Storm

Jesse sat in his father's old chair, fingers tracing the worn leather of James Walker's journal. His father's last known destination before his death had been Finley Cave. Something about that had never sat right - the supposed meeting with Hayes, the convenient discovery of the body. Now, with proof of Hayes's corruption mounting, Jesse knew he had to investigate.

Jesse led Baxter through the thick Ozark forest, the afternoon sun dappling through the canopy. He dismounted well back from the entrance, securing the horse to a sturdy oak before continuing on foot. His boots made no sound on the rocky ground - another skill learned in France that served him well now.

The cave's massive mouth gaped before him, over fifty feet high. Two men in suits stood guard, Thompson submachine guns strapped over their shoulders. Jesse knew he wasn't going to get in that way. His father had shown him something years ago, a secret entrance covered by wild grapevines snaking up the limestone.

Jesse made his way there pushing aside thick curtains of ivy. The narrow opening appeared, barely wide enough for a man to squeeze through. He pulled out his trench knife and proceeded carefully into the darkness.

The passage twisted like a snake's belly, forcing Jesse to crouch low. Water dripped somewhere in the darkness as he navigated by touch more than sight.

Voices echoed through the passage system. Jesse pressed himself against the wall, listening to footsteps pass nearby. "Watch it you idiot," one voice warned. "Lighting a cigarette here will kill us all."

Following the sound of activity, Jesse emerged into a massive chamber. His jaw clenched at the sight - five enormous copper stills, bigger than any he'd seen before, even Bill's operation seemed tiny in comparison. Men in suits moved between them, checking gauges and adjusting valves. This was no backwoods operation - this was on an industrial scale.

"When's the lawman supposed to show?" one man asked, his voice carrying across the chamber.

"He'll be here soon enough," another replied. "Got our new orders from St. Louis."

"Man's always so damn nervous when he comes around here," the first man said. "Fidgeting and looking over his shoulder like he expects the devil himself."

"Wouldn't you be?" the second man scoffed. "Way I see it, that's just good sense. He's got more to lose than most if this operation goes south."

Jesse's fingers tightened around his knife handle until his knuckles went white. "You son of a bitch," he whispered, rage building in his chest. "You killed my father over this." The pieces fell into place - Hayes working with the mob, his father discovering the operation, the 'accidental' death. His blood boiled at the betrayal.

Moving back through the shadows, Jesse's mind was made up. Hayes would answer for his crimes - tonight.

* * *

Night had settled over the town when Jesse took his position in the shadows across from Hayes's house. The rising wind carried the promise of a storm, stirring the trees and scattering loose leaves across the empty street. The air felt heavy with electricity, matching the tension in Jesse's chest as he watched the yellow light of the sheriff's study window.

Inside, Hayes sat at his desk, papers scattered before him under the warm glow of an oil lamp. He leaned back in his chair and massaged his temples, the strain of reading in dim light taking its toll. A sudden creak from the sitting room caught his attention, making him pause mid-motion.

Hayes's eyes darted to his study doorway, peering into the darkness beyond. Rising slowly, he moved to the wall where his gun belt hung, drawing his revolver with practiced ease. The leather of his holster creaked as he pulled the weapon free and thumbed back the hammer.

Edging cautiously into the darkened sitting room, Hayes swept his gun across the shadows. Finding nothing, he approached the front of the house where the storm door rattled against its frame. He checked through the window before stepping out to secure it, latching both the storm door and main entrance firmly.

As Hayes turned back toward his study, the barrel of Jesse's revolver pressed cold against his temple.

"Jesse?" Hayes's voice shifted from shock to anger. "Have you lost your damn mind, boy?"

"Move," Jesse commanded, gesturing toward the study.

"You put a gun to my head? In my own home?" Hayes's face flushed red with rage as he walked stiffly toward the study. "After everything we've been through, everything your daddy and I-"

"My father's exactly why I'm here," Jesse cut him off.

Hayes settled into his chair, his hands gripping the armrests white-knuckled. "You better start explaining yourself right quick, son, before I forget our history."

"This concerns my father, your so-called 'brother' - the man you killed."

Hayes's face twisted with fury and disbelief. "The hell are you talking about, Jesse? I'd sooner shoot myself than harm James! Been wearing out boot leather trying to find who did."

"Still your tongue," Jesse snapped, unconvinced. "Lord knows I fought against believing it, you being close as kin, practically my uncle."

Hayes opened his mouth but Jesse cut him off. "Keep quiet!" The revolver trembled slightly in Jesse's grip, a detail that didn't escape Hayes's notice, making him press his lips together, though anger still burned in his eyes.

"Found me a letter in Father's desk," Jesse continued, his voice rough with emotion. "Spoke of meeting you near Finley Cave on the day of his death, said he aimed to 'settle accounts once and for all.'"

Jesse leaned forward slightly. "Then I witnessed you and Wilcox, that bank serpent, dealing like Judas in front of the courthouse. Watched Richmond pat your shoulder during the Weber trial - familiar as a farmer with his favorite mule. The same Richmond grinding my family under his heel."

Thunder cracked outside as Jesse's finger tightened on the trigger. "Today brought discovery of a shine operation vast as Dante's circles in Finley Cave. Heard talk of taking orders from a lawman." The hammer of the revolver clicked like fate itself. "What words you got to match these deeds, Marcus?"

Hayes leaned forward, his weathered face earnest in the lamplight, though anger still tightened his jaw. "Listen close, son. Your daddy and me were working together, building a tight case against Richmond's outfit."

Jesse's grip tightened on his revolver. "You're asking me to swallow poison and call it medicine?"

"That letter you found - James called me out to Finley Cave. Said he had evidence that would bring Richmond's whole house of cards tumbling down." Hayes's voice found its strength. "And what you're telling me about that shine operation - well, that's the missing piece we've been hunting. It completes the puzzle."

"What manner of puzzle?" Jesse's eyes narrowed like a rifle sight.

"Your daddy spotted something peculiar - bank claiming honest folk weren't making payments. James was set to testify for John Weber." Hayes shifted in his chair. "Weber and your daddy, they'd ride into town together every month. James watched John hand over every dollar that bank claims never existed."

"Then why didn't you speak up at Weber's trial?" Jesse demanded. "You knew Father went with him to make payments."

Hayes's anger softened slightly. "What good would it have done? Your daddy was gone, couldn't testify. My word alone? Circumstantial at best. Would've just marked me as trouble without helping John one bit."

Lightning flashed outside as Hayes continued. "After they took Weber's place, your daddy came to me. We started digging, quiet-like, but couldn't get proper proof. Then James sends word to meet him at Finley Cave - said he'd found something big as creation. When I got there..." Hayes's voice cracked. "Found him there, dead. Never knew what he meant to show me."

Hayes reached slowly toward his desk drawer, his weathered hands trembling slightly. "I pressed on Wilcox something fierce. He held firm till the bank turned on his own kin's farm by the cave. That's when he passed me this here paper."

Jesse caught the folded paper Hayes tossed across the worn oak desk. The yellowed document crackled as he opened it, revealing a meticulously typed list of farms within three miles of Finley Cave - including the Weber place and his family's land. His jaw tightened as he noticed familiar names, good people who'd worked that ground for generations.

"They're grabbing every piece of land round that cave," Hayes explained, leaning forward in his creaking chair, careful not to make any sudden moves with Jesse's revolver still trained on him. "That shine operation explains the why of it. Perfect spot - hidden away, defendable as a fort, good water, and corn farmers aplenty. Been laying this trap since before last summer."

Jesse's hand trembled slightly on the gun. The evidence before him challenged everything he'd believed about Hayes's guilt. The anger that had driven him here began to crack, leaving confusion in its wake.

"Why didn't you tell me sooner?" Jesse's voice was hoarse, the gun still pointed at Hayes but lowered slightly.

Hayes kept his hands visible on the desk. "Because I couldn't trust anyone, Jesse. Not with Richmond's men watching my every move. Your daddy's death… I've been gathering proof, trying to piece it all together."

Slowly, Jesse eased the hammer down, though the weight of his earlier accusations hung heavy between them. "Marcus, I've done you wrong," he managed finally, his voice rough with emotion. "I should have known better than to think you'd…"

Hayes rose carefully from behind the desk and crossed to Jesse's side, placing a weathered hand on his shoulder. "You're hurting, boy. Looking for answers like a lost lamb. Known you since you were knee-high to a grasshopper - understand that pain better'n most." He squeezed gentle but firm. "Been eating at my soul that I ain't found James's killer yet."

"Least now we see the bank's game clear as day," Jesse said, wiping his eyes with his sleeve. "Gives us chance to set things right."

Hayes nodded. "With what you found up at Finley Cave, I can gather a posse. We'll shut that operation down proper-"

"That path leads to death," Jesse cut in. "Richmond's got strings running to the St. Louis mob. Them cave guards ain't just local boys playing tough."

Hayes's brow furrowed. "Now how'd you come by that particular piece of knowledge?"

"Got my sources," Jesse replied simply. "Best you don't ask more than that."

"Take near a week to get federal boys down here to back our play," Hayes said, running a hand through his graying hair.

"Might be what the situation calls for," Jesse said. "But let's hold that card close till we've played our other hands."

"Smart thinkin', son," Hayes agreed. "And Jesse… next time you need answers, try knocking on my front door first."

"Marcus… might I ask a thing of you?"

Hayes managed a smile. "Name it."

* * *

Jesse guided Baxter through the darkness, the horse's hooves beating a steady rhythm against the packed earth. Only a thin sliver of moon broke through the storm clouds, offering just enough light to make out the path ahead. His jaw tightened - he'd never outgrown his childhood fear of storms.

As he approached the farmhouse, the wind picked up, whipping his coat around him and carrying the sharp scent of coming rain. He quickly led Baxter into the barn, securing him in his stall with fresh hay before heading toward the house.

A massive figure emerged from the shadows near the front porch - the Osage warrior who guarded The Jumping Frog. The man's face remained stoic as he extended a folded note toward Jesse.

Jesse opened it under the porch light, recognizing Rose's elegant handwriting:

"Be careful. My sources inside Richmond Bank say Richmond plans to prevent you from making your final payment. -Rose"

The screen door creaked and clicked shut. Tom and Sarah stepped onto the porch, his mother wrapping her shawl tighter against the rising wind.

"Who's your friend, Jesse?" Sarah asked, eyeing the imposing native.

"Just a friend of a friend, Mama," Jesse replied, tucking the note into his vest pocket. He glanced around the porch. "Where's Mary got to?"

"She went to town with Luke earlier today," Sarah said. "Went for supplies, but they've been gone since late afternoon. Ain't like Mary to be out this long without word. Starting to fret about it."

Before Jesse could respond, the roar of an approaching engine cut through the storm's rumbling. Jesse turned toward the sound of tires racing up their drive.

Luke's car skidded to stop, spraying gravel. Through the windshield, Jesse saw his cousin's battered face - split lip, bloody nose, and a cut on his cheek. Blood soaked the left sleeve of his tailored suit.

"Luke! What happened?" Jesse rushed to help him from the car.

Luke stumbled out, grimacing as he clutched his bleeding arm. "Bunch of thugs got the drop on us… made off with Mary." His words came between ragged breaths. "Tried to stop 'em… one of them shot me."

Tom pushed forward, his face white with fear. "Mary? Where's Mary?" His hands were shaking as he grabbed Luke's lapels. "What'd they do to her?"

"Easy, Tom," Jesse pulled him back, though his own heart was racing. "Let him speak."

Sarah let out a cry behind them. Tom ran and caught her as her knees buckled, guiding her to a porch chair, but his eyes never left Luke, desperate for answers.

"Couldn't make out who they were," Luke winced, reaching into his jacket with his good hand. "Left me with a message… said it's meant for your eyes."

Jesse snatched the bloodied folded paper, hands shaking as he read:

"Don't deliver the final payment to the bank. If you do, your sister dies. If you contact authorities, your sister dies."

The words blurred as rage and fear churned in Jesse's gut. Tom read over his shoulder, his breathing becoming ragged.

"We gotta find her, Jesse," Tom's voice cracked. "They can't… we can't let them…" His words failed as emotion overtook him.

Sarah remained in the chair, her body trembling as silent tears streamed down her face. She stared unseeing into the darkness, as if Mary might materialize from the shadows.

Luke swayed, his good hand bracing against the porch rail as blood dripped from his wounded arm. "I should've done more," his voice broke, tears mixing with the blood on his face. "They came out of nowhere, six, maybe seven of them. I fought back, Jesse, I swear I did." His composure cracked completely. "The way she screamed when they took her… I'll hear that sound till the day I die."

"Tom," Jesse managed, still gripping his cousin's shoulder. "We need to tend to Luke's arm. Can you fetch Mama's sewing kit?"

Tom looked torn between action and staying with Sarah, but nodded stiffly and disappeared inside.

"Mama," Jesse knelt before his mother, taking her cold hands in his. "We're goin' to find her. I promise."

Sarah's eyes finally focused on Jesse, filled with a mother's terror. "My baby girl," she whispered. "They have my baby girl."

Jesse spun toward the Osage warrior still standing silently by the porch. He thrust the letter at him.

"Get this to Rose quick. See if she can track down where they're keeping Mary."

The warrior nodded once, already moving. In seconds, he'd mounted his horse and disappeared into the gathering storm.

12

Firefight

Jesse eased his mother's door shut, his heart heavy. Two days had passed, and still Sarah barely spoke, barely ate. The sound of the storm outside matched his dark mood as he made his way down the hallway to check on Luke.

The guest room door creaked as Jesse entered. Luke lay on the bed, his tailored shirt replaced with one of Jesse's old ones, the left sleeve cut away to accommodate the bandages. The lamp's dim light revealed fresh spots of blood seeping through the white cloth.

"Need to change those dressings," Jesse muttered, gathering fresh bandages from the bedside table.

Luke stirred, wincing as Jesse began unwrapping the old bandages. "How's Aunt Sarah?"

"Same as yesterday. Barely holding on." Jesse examined the stitches he'd sewn two nights ago. The neat, even rows reminded him of France, of battlefield hospitals where they'd had to make do. "These are holding well. Guess some skills you never forget."

"Lucky for me," Luke managed a weak smile.

Jesse cleaned the wound carefully. "Never seen you like that before, the other night. All that emotion." He paused, remembering. "Used to wonder if you felt anything at all, way you kept to yourself growing up."

Luke's eyes clouded. "Guess people can surprise you."

"Suppose they can." Jesse finished rewrapping the arm. "Rest up. I'll bring some soup later."

In the sitting room, Jesse cracked the window despite the storm. The front porch awning kept the rain at bay, and the breeze helped cut through the oppressive humidity. Lightning flashed across the premature darkness - though it was barely afternoon, the storm had turned the day as dim as twilight as he settled into the chair by the window.

Reaching for his pipe, Jesse patted his vest pockets before remembering. "Left it somewhere," he muttered, chewing absently on the pipe stem. The helplessness of their situation gnawed at him as he sat there, unable to act.

Two days. Two days of waiting, of watching his mother cry, of imagining what Mary might be enduring. Jesse stood abruptly, unable to sit still any longer. His boots marked a steady path across the floorboards as he paced.

The sound of footsteps made him turn. Luke emerged from the hallway, his face still bearing the marks of the beating. Jesse hurried to help him to a chair.

"Aunt Sarah's finally resting," Luke said, easing himself down. "The poor woman cried herself to exhaustion."

"Much obliged for lookin' after her," Jesse said, returning to his post by the window. The storm's fury matched his darkening thoughts.

"I should've done more to protect Mary," Luke's voice cracked. "It happened so fast."

"Nothin' you could've done against numbers like that," Jesse said, his jaw clenching.

Luke shifted in his chair, grimacing at the movement. "The other night… I heard you mention Rose. You wouldn't mean the proprietor of The Jumping Frog, would you?"

"I would."

"Now how'd you come to know about that establishment?" Luke's good hand gripped the armrest, betraying his unease.

"Made her acquaintance through mutual friends," Jesse said, turning to face his cousin. "Matter of fact, spotted you there once yourself."

Luke's eyes widened, color draining from his already pale face.

"Pay it no mind," Jesse added. "Everyone deserves a drink now and then."

Luke's tension melted into a nervous chuckle. "Well, seems even the most respectable among us require occasional diversions."

The front door burst open, cutting through their conversation. Tom stood in the doorway, rain streaming off his clothes and forming puddles at his feet.

Tom stepped forward. "Rose's people found her."

"Where're they holding her?" Jesse asked, his voice tight with urgency.

Tom nodded grimly and spoke quietly. "It ain't good news. Richmond's got her at his estate just outside Springfield. He's plannin' to kill her if you make that payment. And he's got mob muscle all over the place."

Jesse pulled Tom further aside, lowering his voice away from Luke. "Reckon this ties back to our railroad endeavors?"

"No," Tom whispered. "Rose checked - they're keepin' the robbery quiet. No feds involved. She figures they can't risk havin' authorities pokin' around that money."

"Then we make sure it never comes back to us," Jesse muttered.

"Robbery?" Luke cut in from across the room. "What's this about a robbery?"

Jesse cleared his throat. "Bank's trying to rob us clean. But they'll learn what happens when you rile highland folk - Mary's coming home."

"You have information about her whereabouts? The identity of her captors?" Luke pressed, trying to sit straighter despite his injury.

"Better you keep your hands clean, cousin. Might need your legal wisdom when dust settles." Jesse walked to his father's desk and retrieved an envelope of money. "Though there is one matter needs tending."

He handed the cash to Luke. "I'm placing our lives and home in your hands. This needs to find its way to Richmond's coffers before they close today. Can you manage that?"

Luke stared at the money, then squared his shoulders with resolve. "Consider it handled."

He grabbed his hat by the door and turned back. "Exercise caution," he said, before stepping out into the storm.

Jesse turned to Tom, his voice tight with determination. "We need help. Know anyone willing to get their hands dirty?"

Tom nodded. "Rose offered us some hands to help. And Virgil said he'd bring backup too."

"Good. Get the truck ready and pull it out front."

As Tom hurried out, Jesse made his way back to his mother's room. He eased the door open, stepping into darkness broken only by lightning flashes. Pulling up a chair beside her bed, he lit the lamp on the nightstand, its warm glow filling the room.

Sarah stared out the window at the raging storm, her eyes red and swollen from crying. "How you holding up, Mama?" Jesse asked softly.

"Not too good." Her voice trembled. "You an' Mary are all I got left in this world. Feels like ever'thing I love is bein' taken away."

"I'll fetch her home, Mama."

She turned to him then, her face set with steel beneath the grief. "You bring the wrath of God upon 'em all, Jesse. Don't let a single one of 'em escape His judgment." Her hand reached up to touch his cheek. "You bring my girl home and you bring my boy home safe as well."

Jesse fought back tears as he nodded. "Yes ma'am. They'll feel the wrath of the Walker family before it's all said and done."

* * *

The truck swayed along the muddy back roads, its passengers gripping whatever they could to stay steady. Jesse looked around at the men gathered beneath the tarp - a mix of Native Americans, former soldiers, and others who'd suffered under Richmond's schemes. The rain hammered against the canvas above them, creating a constant drumming that nearly drowned out the thunder.

"Before we reach our Rubicon," Jesse raised his voice over the storm, "there's something needs saying. What lies ahead's got more danger than a serpent's smile. Anyone wanting clear conscience and clean hands, now's the time. You'll hear no judgment from me."

Joseph, the eldest of Rose's Osage warriors, spoke first. His weathered face caught the dim light filtering through the tarp. "Rose speaks truth about Richmond. He threatens all our ways. We fight now for survival, not just for your sister."

"That's right," Virgil added, adjusting the rifle across his lap. "You done saved my life from them Finley River dogs. 'Sides," he gestured to James and Arthur beside him, "we all done lost somethin' to dat bank of Richmond's. Time somebody stood up to 'im."

The other men nodded in agreement, their faces set with determination. The solidarity of these men, from such different walks of life, struck Jesse deeply. They'd all suffered under Richmond's corrupt empire - Native Americans' livelihood threatened, farmers stripped of their heritage, soldiers returning home to find everything gone.

The truck lurched to a stop, Bill cutting the engine. In the pitch black of late night, the rain intensified, drumming harder against the tarp as lightning split the sky. Jesse checked his weapons as the men prepared to move out into the storm.

"Got my gratitude," Jesse said simply. "Each and every one."

They climbed down from the truck bed into the downpour.

Virgil motioned everyone closer, speaking in hushed tones as rain dripped from their hats and shoulders. "Richmond's place down dis here drive. From what we been seein', he done called in some serious muscle from St. Louis - real professional-like."

Lightning flashed, briefly illuminating the iron gates ahead. Virgil pointed to different positions as he laid out the plan.

"Me an' my boys - James, Joseph, William, Henry - we gonna hit de front, make us some noise. Arthur, Samuel - dat ridge yonder gives ya clean shots at de courtyard. Pick off anybody what gives us trouble." He turned to Jesse and Tom. "Dat leaves you two ta circle 'round back, find Miss Mary while they's focused on us."

Jesse nodded, impressed by the tactical thinking. It wasn't unlike planning assaults in France - create a diversion, then strike the weak point. He checked his weapons one final time as the men split into their groups.

"Good huntin'," Bill whispered, clapping Jesse's shoulder. "If'n any of you fine fellers end up meetin' yer maker tonight, rest 'sured I'll pour out 'nough shine ta float ol' Noah's ark." He cackled softly. "Might do that anyhow."

Despite the tension, several men cracked grins at Bill's gallows humor. They'd need that spirit for what lay ahead.

Jesse and Tom crept through the dense woods, staying low as they circled wide around Richmond's estate. Thunder cracked overhead as they moved between the trees, their boots sinking into the mud with each step.

Through gaps in the foliage, Jesse caught glimpses of Richmond's mansion looming ahead - a massive two-story clapboard structure with white columns and wraparound porches. A tall stone wall surrounded the mansion. The main entrance featured an ornate iron gate where the curved gravel driveway met the road.

Down the main drive, Virgil led his group toward a shallow creek bed that cut along the right side of the property. Days of constant rain had turned the creek into a swift-running stream, but it still offered perfect cover as they worked their way closer to the gate. Two mobsters stood guard, Thompson submachine guns held casually across their chests, tilting their fedoras against the rain as they struggled to keep their cigarettes burning.

Virgil held up his hand, stopping the group. "Need ta take 'em quiet-like," he whispered. "Can't go alertin' the whole place."

Joseph nodded to Henry. "We got this." Both men drew their hunting knives and moved forward through the shadows.

In one fluid motion, Joseph's knife found the first guard's throat. But the second guard turned at the sound, eyes widening as he started to raise his gun. Before he could fire, Henry's knife spun through the air and buried itself in the man's chest. He dropped without a sound.

The natives quickly dragged the bodies into the creek bed, retrieving the tommy guns before signaling the others forward. Virgil rattled the heavy gate - locked tight.

"They carry no keys," Joseph reported.

James stepped up, pulling a leather roll from his jacket. "Stand back." He selected two thin tools and worked the lock with practiced skill. Within seconds, the mechanism clicked and the gate swung open silently.

Virgil and his men reached a small clapboard shed. They pressed against its weathered walls, water streaming down their faces as they assessed the front entrance. Five mobsters huddled under the porch overhang, their submachine guns glinting in the periodic lightning flashes.

Virgil motioned silently - James and William would follow him left while Joseph and Henry broke right. They'd use the line of parked cars for cover. Joesph's grip tightened on his rifle as he prepared to move.

Virgil raised three fingers, then two, then one. They burst from cover, splashing through puddles toward the vehicles. A mobster's shout cut through the rain. Gunfire erupted, muzzle flashes lighting up the night. Virgil's team dove behind the cars as bullets sparked off metal and shattered windows.

The air filled with the distinctive chatter of Thompson guns as both sides exchanged fire. William popped up to take a shot, dropping one of the mobsters. James raised his shotgun, blasting two mobsters who then tumbled down the front steps.

A movement on the second floor caught Joseph's eye. A mobster appeared on the balcony, tommy gun raised toward Virgil's position. Before Joseph could shout a warning, a sharp crack split the air. The mobster jerked backward, Arthur's shot from the ridge finding its mark.

William stood to change position, but a burst of gunfire caught him in the chest. He stumbled backward, a look of surprise on his face as he collapsed into the mud. James tried to reach him but Virgil held him back as bullets chewed up the ground between them.

Samuel's rifle cracked again from the ridge, taking down another mobster. Virgil and the other took cover leaving William's body in the rain-soaked courtyard.

* * *

Jesse and Tom crouched in the creek bed behind Richmond's estate, rain pelting their faces as they watched two mobsters patrol along the back wall. The men walked methodically, tommy guns held ready as they scanned the darkness.

"That trench knife still riding your hip?" Jesse whispered, his hand resting on his own blade.

"Always do." Tom patted his belt. "Like an ol' friend."

"Need to take 'em swift and silent. Can't have one side hearing the other's death rattle."

Tom nodded, his eyes never leaving the patrolling guards. "Ya know, bein' down here in this mud…" Tom's voice grew distant. "Takes me right back to them trenches in France."

"Was thinkin' the same," Jesse replied softly. "That devil's quiet before the whistle screams and all hell breaks loose."

Tom gave a grim nod, understanding in his eyes. They'd both lived through enough of those moments.

Suddenly gunfire erupted from the front of the mansion - the distinctive chatter of tommy guns mixed with rifle shots. The two mobsters at the back gate exchanged looks before quickly abandoning their post. They rushed toward the sound of fighting, boots splashing through puddles as they disappeared around the corner.

"Now's our chance," Jesse said, already rising from the creek bed. "Let's go."

Lightning flashed across the sky as Jesse and Tom sprinted through the downpour toward the back gate. The iron bars loomed before them, padlocked and unyielding. Without a word, Tom braced himself against the stone wall, interlacing his fingers to create a foothold.

Jesse grabbed Tom's shoulders and stepped into his cupped hands. Tom heaved upward as Jesse scrambled for the top of the wall. The rough stone scraped his palms as he pulled himself up, rain streaming down his face.

Rolling onto his stomach atop the wall, Jesse reached down to Tom. Their hands locked together and Jesse pulled while Tom walked his feet up the wall. They both dropped silently into the manicured garden on the other side.

Keeping low, they darted from bush to marble statue, using every bit of cover. The submachine gun felt heavy in Jesse's hands as lightning illuminated the grounds in stark flashes. Tom moved beside him, Springfield rifle at the ready, checking their flanks with practiced precision.

The sound of gunfire at the front of the mansion grew more intense. They reached the back door - solid oak with brass fittings. Jesse pulled his trench knife from its sheath, working the blade into the gap beside the lock. The familiar motions brought back memories of breaking into German bunkers. With a soft click, the lock gave way.

Jesse and Tom slipped inside, water dripping from their clothes onto polished wooden floors. Ornate Persian rugs lined the hallway, leading past gilt-framed paintings and mahogany furniture that spoke of old money.

A mobster rounded the corner, eyes widening at the sight of them. Before he could shout, Jesse's trench knife caught him under the jaw, brass knuckles crushing bone. The man crumpled without a sound. Another guard appeared, but Tom was already moving. His blade found the man's throat as they crashed into a carved side table.

Gunfire from the front of the mansion intensified, bullets punching through windows and splintering wooden frames. Glass shattered as rounds tore through the formal dining room. Jesse and Tom pressed forward, ducking past marble columns.

Two more guards burst from the dining room, pistols drawn. Jesse shoulder-checked the first into an antique vase, following through with brass knuckles that sent teeth flying. The second guard squeezed off a shot that went wide before Tom tackled him. They crashed through double doors into the front parlor just as bullets strafed through the windows. The guard jerked and went limp, caught in the crossfire.

"Upstairs!" Jesse shouted over the chaos. They bounded up the sweeping staircase, boots thundering on hardwood steps. A mobster at the top landing opened up with a tommy gun. Jesse and Tom dove behind the carved banister as rounds chewed into the woodwork.

Tom's rifle cracked and the gunman stumbled backward. Jesse surged up the remaining stairs, catching the wounded man with a savage uppercut that sent him tumbling down the steps.

"Watch it!" Tom shoved Jesse aside as another guard emerged. The man's bullet grazed Tom's shoulder, tearing cloth and flesh. Tom grunted in pain but kept moving, ramming the guard into the wall hard enough to crack plaster.

Jesse and Tom burst through the office door, wood splintering around the brass hinges. Behind an imposing mahogany desk sat Theodore Richmond, his silk suit pristine despite the chaos. Mary struggled against his grip, tears streaming down her face around the cloth gag. His revolver pressed against her temple as he smiled coldly.

Two mobsters flanked the desk, submachine guns trained on Jesse and Tom. Jesse's heart stopped as he recognized the scarred face of one - put he couldn't place where he had seen the man.

"Mr. Walker," Richmond said with a satisfied smile, "it would have been so much simpler if you'd just stayed quiet and allowed my bank to foreclose on your property. But it seems you insist on doing things the difficult way." He tightened his grip on Mary, making her whimper. "Now, do be sensible and put down your weapons."

"Release Mary first," Jesse growled, keeping his tommy gun steady.

"I don't believe you quite comprehend the situation. I am, after all, the one in control here." Richmond's smile widened as the gunfire outside began to fade. "Ah, do you hear that? Your pathetic collection of miscreants has failed. Now comply with my demands, or I shall be forced to end your sister's life in a most unpleasant manner. Namely, I will blow her brains out."

Jesse's mind raced, searching for options as Tom glanced his way, waiting for direction. The cold click of a revolver hammer behind them froze Jesse's blood.

"Lower your weapons, Jesse, and afford Mr. Richmond your

attention." Said a voice from behind.

Jesse turned slowly, disbelief washing over him as he saw Luke standing there, revolver aimed at his head. "You?"

Luke's familiar face twisted into a cruel smile. "Indeed."

Rage and betrayal burned in Jesse's chest as he dropped his weapon. Tom followed suit, his rifle clattering to the floor as he pressed his hand against his bleeding shoulder. Luke stepped past them to stand beside Richmond's desk, and suddenly the pieces fell into place - the scarred mobster, Luke's office, all of it connecting in one horrible moment of clarity.

Jesse's world splintered as Luke's words hit him like physical blows. Each revelation twisted the knife of betrayal deeper. Rain lashed against the windows as lightning illuminated Luke's cold smirk.

"You're the Judas behind Father's death, ain't you? You're the lawman those moonshiners were taking orders from." Jesse's voice shook with rage.

"Quite accurate," Luke's smile unfurled like a serpent's hood. "Though I must admit, shooting myself the other night was rather unpleasant. But necessary - the grieving, wounded hero played so well, didn't it? The tears were a particularly nice touch, I thought."

Mary's muffled sob cut through the room. Tears streamed down her face as she struggled against Richmond's grip.

"You son of a bitch!" Jesse lurched forward, only stopping when Luke's revolver steadied at his head.

"Careful now, cousin." Luke's voice dripped with mock concern. "And yes, I am quite literally the son of a whore, aren't I? Something your precious father never let me forget."

"That's a damn lie and you know it!" Jesse's hands clenched into fists. "Father treated you like his own son!"

Luke's face darkened. "Did he? Do you remember when my Grandmother died, Jesse? I was five years old, thrust into your perfect little family. Oh, how generous Uncle James and Aunt Sarah were, taking in their dead sister-in-law's bastard. The boy with the whore mother and the phantom father."

His voice took on a bitter edge. "They tried so hard to be kind, didn't they? But I saw it in their eyes - the pity, the worry that I'd turn out like my mother, a reprobate. Every Sunday at church, every social gathering, every time someone whispered about 'poor little Luke Walker.'" He spat the name like poison.

"They gave you everything!" Jesse roared.

"They gave me scraps from their table!" Luke shot back. "You had the Walker name, the respect, the future. I had my grandmother's money - my only real inheritance - carefully managed until I could escape to law school. The perfect chance to reinvent myself."

Luke adjusted his silk tie with his free hand. "Then Mr. Richmond offered me something better than family - power. Real power. When your father discovered our operation at Finley Cave…" A cruel smile played across his lips. "The look of betrayal in his eyes… 'Luke, son,' he said, 'whatever's led you here, we can make it right.'"

Luke's eyes took on a distant, almost dreamy quality. "I'll never forget the sound - that sharp crack when I broke his neck with my own hands. The way his body went limp, those eyes still full of that pathetic fatherly concern."

Mary's knees buckled, only Richmond's grip keeping her upright as she wept harder. Jesse's face twisted into something barely human, a sound like a wounded animal tearing from his throat.

"The best part? Playing the grieving nephew afterward. Comforting Aunt Sarah, helping with the farm, being the 'good son' while you were off playing soldier in France. I even intercepted her letters to you - a simple arrangement with the postmaster. Then fabricated stories about sending telegrams searching for you." Luke laughed softly. "Such delicious irony."

Luke's smile widened. "And we're quite aware of your railway enterprise and its acquired capital."

Jesse's eyes widened as Luke reached into his pocket, pulling out a round silver tin. He tossed it to Jesse, who caught it reflexively. His stomach dropped as he saw his initials "JW" etched into the metal - his tobacco tin that he thought he'd lost somewhere else. He must have dropped it during the train robbery.

"How delightfully ironic - attempting to settle debts with purloined funds." Luke deposited the envelope on Richmond's desk with theatrical precision. "I'm afraid your payment never reached its intended destination." He chuckled darkly.

Richmond spoke up, his voice oily. "Since this payment wasn't delivered before closing time, the Walker farm is now legally mine." He jerked Mary roughly, making her cry out through the gag. "And gentlemen, we still require the location of the funds you stole. Otherwise…" He yanked Mary again, and her eyes, red from crying, locked onto Jesse's with desperate pleading.

"You touch one hair on her head-" Jesse's threat cut short as Luke thumbed back the hammer of his revolver with an ominous click.

"Now, now, cousin. Let's be civil about this," Luke said. "Though I must admit, it would be poetic - having you watch her die like I watched Mother waste away. The symmetry is rather appealing."

"Hold your fire!" Jesse raised his hands, his voice breaking. "Just swear to her safety, on whatever honor you got left."

"You have my assurance," Richmond said smoothly, though his grip on Mary didn't loosen.

Jesse swallowed hard, tasting bile. "There's a cave down in the southeast holler of our land. The money is there."

Luke nodded to one of the mobsters. "Assemble some men and retrieve it."

The scarred mobster left without a word. Richmond stood, keeping his grip tight on Mary as he gestured with his revolver. "Shall we take a brief stroll, gentlemen?"

"And Jesse?" Luke added, his voice carrying that same cruel amusement. "Do try to behave. I'd hate for Mary to suffer the same fate as dear Uncle James. Though I must say, breaking a neck becomes easier with practice."

* * *

Jesse stumbled forward through the mud as Richmond, Luke, and the mobsters marched them toward the dark woods. The rain continued its steady pour, and the thunder rolled overhead, lightning illuminating the tears streaming down Mary's face. Tom gripped her hand tightly, trying to offer what comfort he could.

"Seems your word's worth about as much as Confederate money," Jesse said, his voice tight with anger.

Richmond laughed coldly, shifting his umbrella to better shield himself from the rain. "I'm afraid I wasn't entirely truthful."

Mary sobbed harder, and Tom squeezed her hand. The sound of her crying made Jesse's chest ache with helpless rage.

"Are you aware of my holdings in this region?" Richmond gestured broadly with his free hand, the umbrella tilting slightly. "One hundred and fifty acres, to be precise." His smile was vicious in the darkness. "I can assure you that no one will discover your remains out here. You'll simply vanish, and come Monday morning, I will evict your dear mother and acquire your property. That charming farmhouse of yours? It will be demolished by week's end."

He gripped Jesse's shoulder as they moved toward the woods. "Your land will host a substantial distillery operation, generating hundreds of thousands in annual revenue. We'll utilize your existing crops, and once we secure the remaining properties, everything will fall into place quite nicely."

As they neared the woods near the creek bed, rifle shots rang out from behind them. Jesse and Tom dropped to the ground for cover, Tom bringing Mary down with him. A mobster dropped instantly, blood spraying from his chest. The second mobster spun to return fire but a bullet caught him between the eyes, dropping him like a stone.

Luke bolted towards the woods, disappearing into the darkness. Richmond dropped his umbrella, fumbling for the revolver at his waist, but before he could raise it, four shots ripped through his chest, sending him crumpling to the mud.

Virgil emerged from the shadows with Joseph and Arthur, rifles still smoking. "Y'all alright?" Virgil called out.

"We're okay," Jesse said, climbing to his feet. "Pass that rifle here. Got me a Judas to reckon with."

Virgil handed over his Springfield without hesitation. Mary struggled to her feet, mud caking her dress. "Kill 'im, Jesse," she spat, voice raw with fury.

As Jesse shouldered the rifle, Tom grabbed Virgil's arm. "Richmond done sent men to the farm. We gotta stop 'em."

"Done took care of them sorry bastards," Virgil said with a grim smile. "Caught 'em 'fore they could make it to they cars."

Jesse didn't wait to hear more. He plunged into the woods after Luke, rage burning hotter than before.

The creek bed welcomed him with cool water, soaking through his boots as rain poured down in heavy sheets. He moved with skillful precision, each step calculated, Springfield rifle held tight against his shoulder just as it had been in the Argonne. A shot cracked through the darkness like thunder, splintering bark from the tree beside his head. Jesse dove behind a fallen oak, his breath coming in controlled bursts.

"Your European sabbatical should have been permanent, dear cousin!" Luke's voice echoed through the woods. "Left well enough alone!"

"Like you left my father alone?" Jesse fired toward Luke's voice, satisfaction coursing through him at the sound of his cousin scrambling for cover. The rain drummed against leaves overhead, thunder rolling across the sky like God's own fury.

"Your father's antiquated nobility proved his fatal flaw!" Another shot whizzed past, close enough that Jesse felt the displacement of air. "You should have heard him, Jesse. All that talk of family and redemption while I wrapped my hands around his throat!"

Jesse's blood boiled. He fired twice in rapid succession, forcing Luke deeper into the woods. "That what you told yourself when you played the grieving nephew? When you held my mother while she wept?"

"Oh, those tears of hers were delicious!" Luke's cultured tone dripped venom. "This modern age belongs to men of ambition, not sentimental fools clutching their bibles and family values!"

They traded shots until both rifles clicked empty. Jesse tossed Virgil's Springfield aside, hearing Luke do the same. The sound of steel being drawn cut through the rain.

"Shall we settle this like gentlemen then?" Luke called out, his voice thick with bloodlust.

"Ain't nothing gentle about kinslayers," Jesse growled, pulling his trench knife. The brass knuckles still carried the same nicks and scratches from the Argonne.

They circled each other in the rain-soaked clearing, moonlight breaking through storm clouds to illuminate their dance of death. Luke attacked first, his movements refined and precise. Jesse recognized the technique - calculated aggression wrapped in collegiate polish.

"Wrestling champion at university," Luke grunted, driving Jesse back through the underbrush. Their blades clashed with metallic rings that echoed through the woods. "Three years undefeated. Rather fitting that I'll end the James Walker line with such... educated brutality."

Jesse absorbed the attacks, letting muscle memory from the trenches guide him. Luke's knife opened a hot line across his arm, but Jesse barely felt it. He'd felt worse in France.

"That fancy education teach you how it feels to kill a man face to face?" Jesse spat blood from a split lip. "Or was Father your first?"

Luke's face twisted with rage. He launched a series of savage attacks that drove Jesse back toward the creek. "I've learned plenty since then! Like how sweet it felt watching you comfort dear aunt Sarah, knowing I'd killed her husband with these very hands!"

Jesse weathered the assault, giving ground strategically. Luke's technique was perfect, but predictable. Jesse had learned to fight in muddy trenches where rules meant nothing and survival meant everything.

They crashed through the underbrush, trading savage blows that would have made their family weep to witness. Luke seemed to have the upper hand, his collegiate training showing in every movement. But Jesse saw what Luke couldn't - the growing wildness in his attacks, the way anger made his movements just a fraction too wide.

"You're still that same pathetic orphan," Jesse taunted, ducking under a slash. "Trying so hard to prove yourself better than your whore mother!"

Luke roared, abandoning his perfect form for a killing strike. It was the opening Jesse had been waiting for. He slipped inside Luke's guard, just like the hand-to-hand instructors had taught him in training. His trench knife drove up under Luke's ribs with force, the resistance of flesh and bone achingly familiar.

"War taught me something that college won't," Jesse twisted the blade, remembering similar moments in muddy European trenches. "Real fighting ain't got rules like them wrestling matches."

Luke gasped, blood trickling from his mouth and mixing with the rain that spattered his once-pristine suit. His manicured hands clutched weakly at Jesse's shirt, those perfectly maintained fingernails now caked with mud and blood.

"The bank..." Luke coughed, blood staining his expensive silk tie. "They will still... take everything..."

Jesse drove the knife deeper, twisting it. "No, they won't. I sent the payment two ways - through you and through Hayes. Wasn't sure about the Sheriff's loyalty, but figured at least one honest man would see it through." His voice turned bitter. "Trusted you most, being family and all. Guess that was my daddy's weakness showing in me."

Understanding dawned in Luke's eyes, quickly followed by hatred so pure it almost masked the fear of death creeping in. "You think... this changes anything?" Blood bubbled at his lips. "You're still... that self-righteous farm boy... playing at being a man."

"And you're still that lost little boy," Jesse growled, "so desperate to prove himself he killed the only father who ever gave a damn about him. I gave you that money believing blood meant something to you."

Luke tried to laugh, the sound wet and grotesque. "James... was weak... just like you..." His perfectly styled hair now plastered to his forehead, those shrewd lawyer's eyes growing dim. "Should've seen... his face... when he realized... his beloved Luke... was going to kill him..."

Jesse twisted the blade one final time, remembering his father's gentle hands teaching him to plow, to pray, to be a man of honor. "That weakness you saw? That was love, you damned fool. And Hayes proved more faithful than my own blood."

Luke's expression shifted in his final moments - something like realization crossing his features before the darkness took him. His mouth worked silently, perhaps trying to form one last cutting remark, but death didn't wait for clever words. The light faded from his eyes, leaving nothing but an empty shell of the boy who'd once shared Jesse's home and broken bread at the same family table.

Jesse let the body slump to the mud, the rain washing blood from his hands just as it had in war. But this blood felt different - heavier somehow, marked with the weight of kinship betrayed and justice served.

Thunder rolled overhead as Jesse retrieved his rifle, his father's voice echoing in his memory: *"The good Lord tells us to love our enemies, son. But sometimes loving them means allowing God to punish their sin."*

13

Dawn After the Storm

The morning sun painted the eastern sky in shades of pink and orange as Jesse emerged from the woods. The rain had finally ceased, leaving behind that peculiar sweetness that only comes after a storm - a mixture of wet earth, fresh grass, and cleansed air. Steam rose from the ground as the warmth touched the rain-soaked earth, creating a ghostly fog that swirled around his boots.

At the front of Richmond's mansion, Tom, Virgil, and Mary stood waiting. The moment Mary spotted Jesse, she broke into a run, nearly slipping on the wet grass before crashing into him with a fierce embrace. Tears streamed down her face as she clutched him tightly.

"Thank the Lord you're alive!" she choked out between sobs, then pulled back to look at him. "Luke?"

"Dead," Jesse said.

"Good," Mary's voice hardened. "Got what was comin' to him, sure enough."

Virgil approached them, his clothes still wet and muddy from the fight. Jesse noticed fresh blood on his sleeve.

"What's our butcher's bill?" Jesse asked, dreading the answer.

"William and Samuel… dey didn't make it," Virgil said, his voice heavy.

"Old Bill done took Joseph and Henry back to Miss Rose's place wit' de bodies. James caught him some lead - ain't bad as it coulda been, but Arthur done borrowed one of Richmond's automobiles to get him to dat doc we trusts."

Jesse extended his hand to Virgil. "Y'all stood with us like the Three Hundred at Thermopylae. Got no words grand enough for that kind of loyalty."

Virgil clasped Jesse's hand firmly, a hint of a smile crossing his weathered face. "Us Doughboys, we sticks together. Ain't nothin' more to say 'bout that."

With a nod, Virgil turned and walked to one of the mobsters' abandoned cars. The engine roared to life, and he disappeared down the long driveway, leaving behind only tracks in the muddy gravel.

Jesse looked at the muddy driveway stretching out before them, his boots sinking slightly into the wet earth.

"Reckon we best plot our exodus," he sighed, running a hand through his rain-soaked hair.

Mary jingled something metallic, drawing Jesse's attention. In her hand, she held up a set of car keys, a slight smirk playing across her face.

"Now what iron horse might those command?" Jesse asked, though he had a pretty good idea.

"Luke's new Model T," Mary replied, the keys dancing between her fingers. "Left 'em right there in the car."

Jesse reached for the keys, but Mary's grip tightened. She pulled them back just out of his reach, that familiar stubborn look crossing her face - the same one she'd worn since they were kids.

"I'll let ya drive on one condition," she said firmly.

"Do tell?"

Mary's eyes narrowed. "You're gonna tell me 'bout this train business and everythin' else you been up to."

Tom let out a low whistle and shook his head. "Reckon this'll be quite the ride home."

Jesse looked between his sister's determined face and the keys in her hand. After everything that had happened, after all the lies and deception from Luke, he owed her the truth. The whole truth.

"Fair enough," he conceded, reaching for the keys again. This time, Mary let them go. "But promise not to get cross."

* * *

Jesse guided Luke's Model T down the familiar dirt road leading to the Walker farm. Despite the morning sun, the ground remained a sodden mess from days of rain, the Model T's tires sinking deep into the mud. Scattered puddles reflected the clear blue sky above, a deceptively peaceful sight. As they rounded the final bend, Jesse spotted Sheriff Hayes sitting on the front porch with Sarah.

The moment the car came to a stop, Sarah burst from her rocking chair. Her legs, weak from worry and illness, found new strength as she ran to embrace both Jesse and Mary. Tears streamed down her face as she held them close.

"My babies… you're home, both of ya home," she sobbed, clutching them tighter.

"Promised you I would didn't I?" Jesse said softly.

Sarah pulled back, cupping his face in her weathered hands. "Yes ya did. Always keep your word, just like your daddy taught."

Tom and Mary gently helped Sarah back into the house as Hayes approached Jesse, pulling a document from his jacket pocket.

"Well son, reckon your homestead's debt-free," Hayes said, handing him the paper. "Bank's own paper saying you don't owe 'em a wooden nickel."

"Much obliged for making that payment on my behalf, Marcus."

Hayes smiled. "Amazing how cooperative folks get when a sheriff and his deputies show up proper-like in uniform." His eyes drifted to the Model T. "That Luke's fancy motorcar?"

Jesse nodded solemnly.

"Luke's hands were red with Father's blood, Marcus. Confessed it with a smile."

Hayes's face drained of color. "Luke?"

"Spoke it with his own forked tongue. He was that lawman those moonshiners whispered about."

Hayes shook his head in disbelief. "And is he…?"

"Dead by my hand," Jesse said firmly. "If the law requires satisfaction, my hands are ready for your irons."

"Not today, Jesse," Hayes replied. "Way I figure, you just saved me from having to do it myself. Some books just need closing."

Jesse nodded as Hayes walked to his car and drove away.

Inside the house, Jesse guided Sarah to her favorite chair by the window. Sunlight streamed through the lace curtains as he knelt beside her, taking her weathered hands in his.

"Mama, truth's got a bitter taste today," Jesse said softly."Luke was the man who took Father from us."

Sarah's breath caught. "Luke? Our Luke?"

"Yes ma'am. Confessed his sins before…" Jesse paused, steadying his voice. "Before I sent him to his final judgment."

Sarah sat perfectly still, her face a mask of conflicting emotions. Tears welled in her eyes but didn't fall. She looked down at her hands, still clasped in Jesse's.

"All this time," she whispered, her voice thin as thread. "Family killin' family." She shook her head slowly. "James always said blood meant somethin'. Even when Luke's grandma passed, he took that boy in like his own."

She stood suddenly, her movements stiff but determined. "Need some air," she said, her voice tight as a fiddle string. "These walls… they're pressin' in too close right now."

Jesse watched as she made her way to the porch, her shoulders straight despite the weight of this new truth.

Mary guided Tom into the kitchen. "Sit," she ordered, pulling out a chair. "That shoulder needs tendin'."

Tom eased himself down, wincing as Mary helped him remove his bloodied shirt. She worked in silence, cleaning the wound with iodine and warm water. Her touch was gentle but sure as she pressed a clean cloth against the bullet graze.

"Shoulda told me what you boys was up to," she said quietly, not meeting his eyes. "All that moonshinin' and robbin' - coulda got yerselves killed."

"Wanted to keep you safe," Tom replied, his breath catching as her fingers brushed his bare skin. "Though reckon that didn't work out so well."

Mary's hands stilled on his shoulder. "You came for me. Both of ya." She finally looked at him, her eyes bright with unshed tears. "You coulda died, Tom Miller."

"Worth the risk," he said softly.

She finished bandaging his wound, but her hands lingered on his shoulder. "I'm still mad at ya both," she whispered, but there was a softness in her voice that hadn't been there before.

Tom reached up, carefully catching one of her hands in his. "Reckon I'll spend a lifetime makin' it up to ya, if you'll let me."

Mary's free hand came up to touch his face, and then she was kissing him, fierce and desperate. Tom pulled her closer, mindful of his injured shoulder, as she melted against him. When they finally broke apart, both breathing hard, Mary pressed her forehead to his.

"Don't you ever keep secrets from me again, Tom Miller," she whispered against his lips.

He answered her with another kiss.

* * *

Jesse's boots scraped across sun-bleached gravel as he made his way up the familiar path. The early August heat pressed down heavy and thick, but Jesse barely noticed it anymore. Four days had passed since Luke's death, since justice had been served in rain and thunder.

He stopped before his father's headstone, the white marble gleamed under the summer sun. The grass had grown fuller around the base, wild and green like the rest of the cemetery's sloping hillside.

"It's done, Daddy," Jesse said quietly, removing his flat cap. "Luke won't trouble our family no more. Reckon he's standing before a higher court now, explaining why he broke the bonds of blood and trust."

A bead of sweat rolled down his temple, but Jesse didn't wipe it away. "I hate that it came to kinslaying. Know that ain't what you taught us. But sometimes a man's got to do what's right, even when it ain't easy."

The breeze picked up, carrying the distant sound of cicadas. "Farm's safe now. Richmond's bank won't be foreclosing on any more honest folk around here. Mary's talking about planting that north field come spring." He managed a small smile. "She's got your stubborn spirit, that one."

Jesse placed his hand on top of the warm stone. "I kept my promise, Daddy. Protected what's ours. Protected the family." He swallowed hard. "Reckon I'm asking you to keep watching over us, if you can."

He stood there a moment longer, feeling the weight of duty lift from his shoulders like morning mist burning off in summer sun. Then he placed his cap back on, turned, and walked away, leaving his father to rest easy in the knowledge that the Walker name - and all it stood for - would endure.

* * *

The Jumping Frog was silent save for the scratch of Rose's pen against paper. The lanterns cast a warm glow across the empty bar as she worked, her dark hair falling forward as she wrote. Jesse's boots echoed on the wooden floor as he approached, each step stirring up the settled dust.

"Burning midnight oil?" he asked, noting the stack of receipts and ledgers spread across the polished bar top.

Rose looked up, a smile playing at her lips, her fingers absently toying with the pen. "Numbers don't sleep, cher. Someone's got to keep le bon temps from running wild on the books."

Jesse settled onto a barstool, the familiar wood creaking beneath him. "Came to offer proper thanks - for the intelligence and the reinforcements. Not many'd risk dancing with devils for neighbors' sake."

"My people knew the price," Rose said softly. "They chose their path, every soul among them."

"Good men. They'll be remembered," Jesse said softly.

Rose set down her pen, the metal tip clicking against the wood. "Them Finley boys are stirring up trouble like storm crows. Word is they're gathering numbers."

"The Finley boys gathering strength?" Jesse's voice held the quiet tension he'd learned to recognize before a storm. "Like vultures circling."

"Pay them no mind," Jesse said. "I've got plans laid for those boys. They'll learn the price of bringing trouble to these hills."

Rose studied his face in the lamplight, her eyes searching his, reading the determination there like a book. "You're cut from different cloth, Jesse Walker. Most men who cross my threshold are hunting whiskey or women. But you..." She leaned forward slightly, close enough that he caught the faint scent of jasmine. "You see things others miss. You think three moves ahead."

Jesse reached into his vest and placed an envelope on the bar, the paper thick with bills. "Two thousand dollars. Small price for loyalty like yours."

Rose's fingers brushed the envelope. "Non, keep your money, cher. Smart business says future discounts will serve better than quick cash. My mama didn't raise no fool."

"Deal," Jesse said with a slight smile, appreciating her business sense. "Should we write up a contract to seal it?"

Rose stood, moving around the bar with fluid grace. She took his hand in hers, her skin warm against his callused palm. "Down in New Orleans, we seal deals with something stronger than paper."

She led him toward the back room, turning to wrap her arms around his neck, her touch sending electricity through his war-weary bones. As their lips met, Jesse reached behind him and closed the door, shutting out the world beyond and all its troubles, if only for a little while.

The End

About the Author

You can connect with me on:

https://www.jacobsansoucie.com

https://www.facebook.com/jsansoucie.author

Subscribe to my newsletter:

https://www.jacobsansoucie.com